‘I bet we coul thing we both e

‘What did you have in n

‘It’s way too early in the night for me to tie myself down to anything specific.’

‘You’ve got an answer for everything, Ms Devine. Sadly it’s too late in the night for me to stay on and find out what you’ll tie yourself down to. Or tie yourself up with. It’s been…interesting.’

He leant a hand on her shoulder and leaned down for the obligatory goodbye cheek-kiss. He smelled product—perfume, hairspray, cosmetics. He touched smooth skin. He let his lips linger for a second too long to be strictly platonic. He curled his other arm round her waist, drawing her closer into him. Her body was soft and nestled perfectly, and he moved his lips to her other cheek. But her lips were in the way, so he placed his kiss there. Just one.

She. Was. So. Hot.

Dear Reader

When Tara Devine first burst onto the page even *I* was taken aback by her sass! Every time she met a challenge she climbed right over it—in her highest, most inappropriate heels. Sometimes I had no idea how she badly she would behave, but one thing was for sure: when she met her match, the feral cat would turn into a kitten. Getting to that stage was never going to be easy, and only a very tough guy showing her very tough love would cut it.

Enter one super-sure, super-hot Michael Cruz. He's seen more than enough of life to see right through Tara. But what he does see hooks him. And even though she pushes him to his very limits, and brings out every chest-thumping, testosterone-pumping part of him, he's her guy and he's prepared to hold on until all the champagne's been drunk and the party's over.

I truly loved these characters. I loved their hot sex and their love story. And I so admired Michael for the patience he was prepared to show. Falling in love with love is easy. But playing the long game and putting yourself second is what really counts.

I hope my very first Modern Tempted™ rocks you the way it rocked me. To be part of this wonderful world of writers and readers sharing the eternal quest for eternal love is the best feeling ever!

With my warmest wishes

Bella x

DRESSED TO THRILL

BY

BELLA FRANCES

Published in Great Britain 2014
by Mills & Boon, an imprint of Harlequin (UK) Limited,
Eton House, 18-24 Paradise Road, Richmond, Surrey, TW9 1SR

ISBN: 978-0-263-91150-3

Harlequin (UK) Limited's policy is to use papers that are natural, renewable and recyclable products and made from wood grown in sustainable forests. The logging and manufacturing processes conform to the legal environmental regulations of the country of origin.

Printed and bound in Spain
by Blackprint CPI, Barcelona

Unable to sit still without reading, **Bella Frances** first found romantic fiction at the age of twelve, in between deadly dull knitting patterns and recipes in the pages of her grandmother's magazines. An obsession was born! But it wasn't until one long, hot summer, after completing her first degree in English Literature, that she fell upon the legends that are Mills & Boon® books. She has occasionally lifted her head out of them since to do a range of jobs, including barmaid, financial advisor and teacher, as well as to practise (but never perfect) the art of motherhood to two (almost grown-up) cherubs.

Her eclectic collection of wonderful friends have provided more than their fair share of inspiration for heroes, heroines and glamorous locations, and it was while waiting to board a flight home after a particularly lively holiday that the characters for her first competition success in *So You Think You Can Write*, were born.

Bella lives a very energetic life in the UK, but tries desperately to travel for pleasure at least once a month—strictly in the interests of research!

Catch up with her on her website at www.bellafrances.co.uk

DRESSED TO THRILL is Bella Frances' debut book for Mills & Boon® Modern Tempted™ and is also available in eBook format from www.millsandboon.co.uk

DEDICATION

For Margaret Isabella Mustard, who loved literature and life.
Governess, teacher, farmer's wife, mother and grandmother.
Thank you.

CHAPTER ONE

TARA MARIE FITZPATRICK DEVINE knew how to behave badly. Very badly. She made it her business to work hard, play hard and then read the hard online copy of her triumphs. It was quite simply the most delicious way to promote herself in the dog-eat-dog world of international fashion. And tonight—the culmination of a whole season of glamorous graft—tonight, her wild streak was shining like neon body paint in a nightclub-dark room.

'*But what am I going to do*?'

Barely aware of the feet that drummed beside hers under the table in the shady booth, Tara dipped into her clutch and pulled out her compact. Another streak of siren-red over her pout while she was still sober enough to care.

'You'll be fine,' she managed to say, looking at her reflection in the tiny mirror.

The thick slicks of liquid eyeliner were almost perfect—crazy that she had never rocked this look before—it was so, *so* burlesque!

'But I'm sure he'll be on his way here next! And if he catches me here…after I told him I was going straight home…'

Tara replaced the lipstick in its little case. Honestly, there was no getting through to this girl.

'Fernanda.'

She swept a glance from the now resting silver platforms to the mouthwateringly beautiful face of Fernanda Cruz—the sexiest Spanish teenager to grace the runways and the tabloids in a decade. Her brown mane hung sexily over one eye and her fuchsia silk mini-dress rode high on endless thighs. The girl looked as if she had never even heard of the word carbohydrate.

'What?'

Tara pointed her lipstick at her.

'You need to stop this. First of all, you're not even sure if he'll definitely turn up. Secondly, if he does... and—let's face it—it is quite likely, then you need to stand up to him. Tell him to get out of your life and stop acting like the overbearing, macho pain in the ass that he is.' She flipped open the compact again and checked her slightly wonky teeth for lipstick, rubbing at them until they squeaked. 'It's not as if you've done anything wrong, Fernanda. It's only an after-party! '

'But you don't understand. My brother Michael rules the family. If he *is* here, I'm...' She mimed being garrotted.

'And *he* has to realise that a life in fashion these days means you have to promote yourself—be seen, get papped, kiss Harry...'

'But I'm his baby sister, Tara! And he hates it. Hates all of it. He wants me to study to be an accountant or something. He thinks models are airheads and designers are fakes.'

Tara's snapped her clutch closed with a little more attitude than was necessary. She knew all about the über-dominant Michael Cruz, Fern's brother and legendary King Machismo. Ten hours earlier, as Fernanda had sublimely showcased Tara's funkiest spring/summer dresses on the runway of her London show, her sickeningly handsome brother had sat in the front row, looking as bored as if he were watching paint dry—the dull shades.

And, though no one had dared tell Tara at the time, the press had been all over it. Photos of him in his immaculately tailored suit, with his perfectly masculine jaw and utterly uninterested expression had hit every online fashion site within moments. Thank heavens his other sister Angelica had shown enough enthusiasm for the whole row. And had been kind enough to drop that she was 'considering' commissioning Tara to design her wedding dress. That just about made up for the arrogance of the man!

'Fern, honey, we've worked hard. Our careers are just taking off. For me, this party is as important as the show. And for you it's what you've been looking forward to for the last month. And we've got it all to do again in two weeks' time in Paris! *Cha-ching!* So if he is here we'll tell him to…to go and count his own beans—and we'll mingle and dance and see what column inches we can capture. Come on!'

She grasped Fern's hand and pulled her to her feet. All six feet of her size zero frame only served to highlight Tara's own whipped cream curves. *Fattest woman in fashion. Overeater von Tease.* Yep, she'd heard them all. And sometimes it hurt—of course it did. But she'd learned long ago that even if she ate air and drank dew she was only ever going to be voluptuous. So she'd put her voluptuousness to good use—she knew how to enhance a cleavage and minimise a belly better than any bra or pair of magic pants.

And, now that the fashion elite had begun to show interest, getting some mainstream press was her next mission. Hence the headline-grabbing dress from her show—she'd styled it *The Seven-Year Bitch: Marilyn meets Madonna*. Though maybe it *hadn't* been the best idea to go this short when there was nothing surer than a cringe-worthy 'getting into the limo badly' photograph appearing in the morning's news feed. More column inches, and even more reasons for Team Devine back home to decry her. Devine girls were supposed to put up and shut up—two of her weakest skills…

The DJ changed and the music turned darker. Tara saw Fern head onto the dance floor with some up-and-coming young cutie and wandered off herself into the throng, smiling and air-kissing the other bottom-of-the-food-chain celebrities. She snagged a glass of champagne from a passing tray and moved back out to the foyer—keen to avoid having to chat with her Dutch financier, easily the most boring man on earth. But when her breath seemed to catch as a gulp of fizz hit the back of her throat, and the faces of the crowd all turned, she realised that someone *very* A-list had just arrived.

Everything in Tara Devine's life happened at a million miles an hour. Her brain processed thoughts that her mouth duly delivered. Which sometimes led to problems. Like when she didn't actually *know* what she'd just said or done until two seconds too late. But here—now—she felt as if she had slipped into slow-mo. She watched, transfixed, as the foyer seemed almost to fade and there, stalking along the red carpet, was the arrogant alpha himself. Michael Cruz. Incorporated.

As the camera flashes whited out the space he turned his head slightly, as if a mildly irritating noise had sounded. Now that she could see him clearly, she saw he was as tall as she had imagined, his physique as perfect. And, though she rarely dressed men, she just knew what lay under the cut of cloth on his back. The ripple of muscle over the perfect masculine ratio of shoulders to waist was flawless.

One hand was at his hip, pushing back his jacket, and the perfect illumination of a white silk-linen shirt gleamed. He turned, paced, and took something handed to him by one of his security team. He slipped it into his pocket, seemed to search out the faces closest to him, and then…

And then a flash of intensely dark eyes landed on her. He scanned her, and her heart raced the moment his gaze probed and zoned over her. His eyes narrowed as they landed on her chest and she instinctively lifted her arms to shield herself. He turned full body to face her as he continued to stare, his eyes sliding down, over and up her legs.

The cameras whirred and flashed, people were talking, calling out to him, capturing his appraisal of her. And then, with what seemed infuriatingly like a condescending smirk, he turned away, dismissing her.

Tara felt colour rush up her chest and burn her cheeks—the stab of childhood sensitivities all over again. It had been a long time since anyone had pierced her armour. And that made her even angrier—how *dared* he? She made to step forward, to tell him what she thought of him—him and his dull, dark, bespoke suit. He was here in the hub of one of the most creative cities in the world, at one of the most exciting times—

when the eyes of the fashion media were trained upon young talent—and he was being openly dismissive of anything other than twenty-four-carat conservatives just like himself.

She had checked him out—the media darling, yet another poacher turned gamekeeper whose definition of art was as narrow as his totally on-trend, no-risk tie. There was no way anyone other than the beautiful people would get a foothold in *his* world. Old money and limb length spoke more than any genuine talent. As far as she could see.

As if to prove her point, a little posse of coltish runway girls circled him, giggling and preening and flashing their thigh-gaps like currency. He brightened and slung arms round two who snuck right under his 'Daddy's home' embrace. Their coquettish display was vile. Sometimes the sisterhood let itself down *so* badly.

'Tara, *querida*! How lovely to see you again.'

Tara turned to see the third member of Club Cruz glide her way towards her. The outrageously elegant Angelica: dream customer and media-savvy goddess of style. Oh, yes. Let the Lord be thanked for the double X chromosomes in the procreation of generation Cruz.

'Angelica!'

Air-kiss, air-kiss and smug glare right over to the arrogant alpha himself. He caught her look and made no effort to hide his calm assessment of the scene. Stood with his adoring troupe, relaxed and controlled. And who could blame him—the way they were practically licking the air around him?

'Angelica, you look beautiful—as ever. Let me see.' Tara stepped back to scan the perfect ensemble, 'You wear couture so well. It's a shame your brother is rocking the boring businessman look, though.'

Angelica laughed lightly and preened politely, linking her arm in Tara's and stepping into the party. 'Michael is putting up with this for me. He doesn't really like the scene any more. But he does enjoy some of the benefits.'

She flicked her eyes to where he stood, acknowledging his current difficulties with amused acceptance.

'This is the third party we've been to and his ego must be bigger than the bar bills. All these beautiful young girls and so few men for them to flirt with. Well, men who like women, that is.'

Tara scanned her fellow partygoers, nodding her agreement. There was more oestrogen in the room than you could shake a fluffy pink wand at. The legions of gay best friends didn't quite boost the already depleted testosterone levels. Even the men in the celebrity underclass were over-preened, with their shaped, tinted brows and oily orange complexions. Really, *really* not a turn-on.

Tara's men were edgy, dark, beta. And invariably in her past. The last real relationship she'd had, with a sensitive, eyeliner-wearing musician, had been during college. The relationships she had now were with champagne and investors. Oh, and the media. Her biggest flirt of all.

'I was wondering if you had seen Fernanda, actually.'

Angelica's tone still had its feather-lightness but Tara could sense a little edge of concern.

'I thought she was staying home, but maybe she has come here with you?'

Tara looked around. Fern hadn't been with her for

quite some time now. 'She *is* here—she went to dance. But if she knows Michael's here she'll be hiding out in the toilets. She had a major meltdown earlier. He must have some hold over her.'

Angelica steered them through to the dance floor, smiling as she passed the partygoers and securing them two glasses of champagne from a conveniently placed table.

'He means well—just worries about her because he is responsible for her. It was never easy for him, being guardian to two orphaned girls.'

She patted her arm as Tara vaguely recalled their back story. Something about him halting his own highly successful model/actor/presenter career when his mum and stepdad were killed in a car crash. Overnight he'd gone from number one Euro party boy to serious, silent and sober. What was it her Irish granny used to say? 'A young tart an old nun makes.' Or something like that. Yes, there was no doubt that his condescending aura was just reformist hot air.

'He thinks everyone in fashion is self-serving and nasty or stupid—because he had such a bad experience when he was younger. You should meet him. Help him put his mind at rest. Oh, and we must have that chat about my dress.'

The very words Tara had been longing to hear. She swallowed her gushing mouthful of thank-yous and smiled coolly. 'Of course. Any time you like. I won't be heading to Paris for a week.'

'Lovely…' Angelica sounded distracted. She unlinked her arm and squeezed her hand. 'I think we should go and find Michael. Maybe you can convince him to stay on here while I take Fernanda home. Discreetly.'

She nodded to where Fern, locking lips with her cutie, was swaying in time to some bassy, carnal music. The fact that she didn't seem to care who saw her grind her hips and lose herself in his mouth kind of screamed that she had kissed goodbye her inhibitions along with several glasses of booze.

Angelica rolled her eyes ever so slightly. 'He won't like it if she's been drinking. He's so protective of her, and it would save a load of heartache if he never had to know.'

Actually, Tara thought that a hell of a lot more heartache would be saved by telling him where to get off—but each to their own.

She squeezed Angelica's hand back. 'I'm on it.'

Helping her friend and getting more into Angelica's good books made a whole lot of sense, too. The only downside was that it was going to mean actually communicating with the grade A-is-for-ass, macho man. What on earth did they have in common? Spain's one-time boy idol, all grown-up and gone cerebral. Who only spoke in words of five syllables in the language of the super-successful.

Maybe it would be simpler if she dropped her clutch and twerked for him. It was rumoured that he still spoke *that* particular language, and maybe then she'd be able to hold his attention long enough for his sisters to get out and away from his overbearing presence.

She had. She'd escaped—or rather, she'd plotted and executed her plan. Walked away when the time was right. And if she could do it any woman could. It was the best thing that had happened to her. *Ever.* Honestly. When she ruled the world she'd arrange for all the arrogant bullies to be herded together and thrown in a pit. And Michael Cruz would be the perfect trophy for the top.

She stomped along, in the wake of Angelica's smooth glide, back to where Michael and his guardette of honour were still lending their eye-blinding beauty to the club photographer. She watched a couple of the better-known runway girls strike poses and got the feeling he wasn't really keen to play any more. But his smile, when he used it, was as dazzling as his sisters'—and, heaven help her, for a moment she could only stare at the masculine beauty of it all.

And then he turned it on Angelica, and warmth crept over his face. So he had a heart?

He eased himself away from one photo op right into another as he greeted his sister. Then he distanced himself from all the white noise as he guided her—only her—with a proprietorial hand on the small of her back, to the bar. Was he being a deliberate jerk or did he truly not know that Tara was behind them?

She could really take it or leave it. This whole, keeping up with the Cruzes, thing. It was taking her well away from where she wanted to be. There were some very interesting new faces and Mr Arrogant had diss'd her twice already—three times if you counted the show today.

She was just about to let them all get on with it when she saw him turn round. Not fully round, but grudgingly, and then, as if he was giving alms to the poor, he gestured that she should catch up with them.

If there was a DEFCON higher than one she might just have reached it. Who the hell did he think he was?

Did every female he met just fall at his feet, or—worse—into line? Not this one. He might look like the man of everyone else's dreams, but he was her personal idea of a nightmare come to life.

'Tara. I don't think we've properly met.'

He didn't think they'd properly met? Really?

She could just see Angelica's dazzling smile through the haze of red that had fallen around her. *Play it cool, play it cool. Don't give him the control. Don't make a fool of yourself.*

She lifted the glass she was almost crushing in her hand and took a long sip.

He gave a little indulgent, half-cocked smile and then walked towards her slowly, hand extended. 'I'm Michael—Angelica's brother. And Fernanda's. Pleased to meet you.'

Oh, he was good. But she was better. She paused, set her drink with very deliberate care on little elbow-height table closest to her, and turned back to face him.

'Yes, I'm sure you are. You were at my show today.' Just in case he thought he would try to gloss over his rudeness. 'You didn't really seem to get it. Fashion not your thing?'

Well, he probably didn't have a lot of women launching conversations with insults, so that might explain his slight double-take. But he covered it well and took her hand. A very warm, very appropriate handshake. No crushing, just firm and male. Very, *very* male.

His eyes bored right into hers. Combative. He let go of her hand. 'Yes, you're absolutely right. I've sat through quite a number of runway shows this week. Wouldn't say it's been the best use of my time, but…it filled a few hours.'

'And created a few million for our economy,' Tara added, sweet as the pie she'd like to throw in his face.

And it was such a yawningly attractive face. Some might even get swept up in the masculine brilliance of the angled cheekbones and defined jaw. Eyes that were slightly almond-shaped and as fathomless as his mood. Lips that were full and dark red, but too hard to be feminine. Lips that she suddenly imagined could give a whole load of pleasure.

Dangerous. Oh. Yes.

She swallowed and forced her thoughts back on track. 'I often think some people forget just how much is involved in the creation of one dress.' She fingered the skirt of her own, unintentionally inviting his appraisal.

Damn, but he didn't think twice about giving it. Was there no end to the gall of the man?

'We were both thrilled to be at your show, Tara. Your designs really are beautiful. And you have the perfect body to show them off.'

Angelica's sparkling tones cut through the heavy air that was swirling between them. 'You are so wonderfully hourglass. You know, I was reading the other day that we are all turning into rectangles. Can you imagine? Straight up and down. No waists to speak of. No wonder you are the toast of the week, sweetie. All us skinnies want to look as feminine as you. Isn't she just adorable, Michael? Oh, look, there's the photographer. We must give him a snap. Michael—you there, arm round Tara. Perfect.'

Angelica buzzed and fluttered and placed herself on Tara's other side as the cameras flashed. And even though she was still fizzing at the easy way he was glossing over his arrogance Tara knew that now wasn't the time to challenge.

Because now he was moving right into her space, extending his arm. Even as her eyes fell on the mouth that twisted into that slight smirk she had just seen. Even if this time the smirk was eclipsed by the pure male sensuality of his lips. And, though she hated that predictable shadowy stubble, defined jaw look, her eyes widened as the up close and personal space of Michael Cruz became shared with her.

She felt his arm circle her waist and draw her to his right side. Firmly. He held her firmly—as if he had every right to wrap his big arm around her and pose her in the camera glare. As if it was totally fine for him to pull her so close to his body and cause fireworks in her nerve-endings. Could everybody see what she was feeling? How embarrassing! Since when was Tara Devine reduced to a puppet by anybody?

She really didn't want to run with that particular thought…

His grip on her waist was tight and unequivocal. She was just a full-fat version of the calorie-free hors d'oeuvres he'd sampled five minutes earlier. And she hate, hate, *hated* that he could do that to her.

Michael felt sure the muscles in his face would spasm any moment now. After the day he'd had, these brutal after-parties were the last thing he needed. But what the hell? He saw Angelica so little that he could stomach hanging out here, since it seemed to be such a big deal to her. Though he hadn't figured on winding up next to this pocket Miss Whiplash: Tara Devine, wildest little firecracker in the box, renowned for her partying, her comic book curves and her utter lack of self-control.

But more to the point—he scanned the room—thankfully Fernanda had been smart enough to leave all this well enough alone. At least she'd been as good as her word and stayed home. And, despite begging him to let her model this week, she seemed to have retained some of the self-control he'd spent the last sixteen years drilling into her. She was young, she was naïve. And she was allying herself to the vacuous people in this awful industry.

He'd be damned if the sense and intelligence she was blessed with would be wasted on all of this. The place was awash with drugs and drink—these parties always were. He'd had more than his fair share back in the day. And he'd be a fool to think there wouldn't be predators trying to get his sister hooked up in it.

He glanced down at the mini sex bomb tucked beneath his arm. She seemed to have burst onto this scene overnight—and wasn't it just typical that his two sisters found her so 'engaging'. This woman had her own look, all right—strawberry blonde hair with strange streaks of platinum and gold, combed and pinned in a kind of soft beehive—not his thing at all. He could see the curve of her throat as it met the creamiest, most flawless skin of her décolletage. The swathe of ivory satin that skimmed the most talked-about society breasts just enhanced them even further, and he dropped his eyes to take them in again.

What the hell? He was a man.

Angelica was right. Tara's waist, now that his hand had relaxed and splayed out against her hip, was actually much smaller than he'd thought when he'd ever thought about it—which was never. And her hips in that skirt—what little there was of it—were soft and round. The whole look reminded him of someone. Someone very feminine. Very sexy. She'd turned, was looking up at him, and her eyes were so blue, outlined in thick black make-up that she just didn't need. Her lips… The reddest, fullest most swollen pout of a mouth he could remember seeing. She was saying something.

'Yes, Fernanda is an amazing model. She has potential to be world-class—a real supermodel. I've booked her for another week. For Paris.'

The fog in his head suddenly cleared. If Fernanda thought he was letting her loose into this circus again she was out of her mind. He'd indulged her notions this once—let her get it out of her system. But no way was she making a career out of this—not when she had the potential to do something worthwhile with her life.

Time for a little distance.

He leaned in to whisper in Tara Devine's ear. 'You'd better *un*book her, then. No way will my sister be working for you, next week or any other.' He smiled as he spoke his words right into her ear, felt her stiffen. He lingered a little longer, and could have sworn she shivered. 'I don't know what she told you, but she has more important things to do than walk up and down wearing a bunch of crazy clothes.'

'Wow, you really *are* a control freak!' Tara hissed at him out of the corner of her mouth, even while she pouted and posed.

She was playing her coy little games for the snappers. The men in the room—the men who weren't caught up in this fashion nonsense—were all posturing, their eyes trained right at her and her frankly ridiculous curves.

She smiled at them, turned in his grasp and cupped his cheek. 'What are you so afraid of? That she'll actually enjoy herself?'

She leaned right into his ear as she spoke and he felt her lips brush his skin and the press of her breast on his arm. So she wanted to play? He could live with another minute of her company if it taught her a lesson.

He caught her wrist, brought her insolent hand down sharply behind her, so that her back arched into him and the spill of those creamy breasts was even more obvious. She let out a little gasp and he trailed his eyes super-slowly right over her smooth silky skin. The bodice of her satin dress was *so* low and his view was *so* good. And damn it if the slow smirk he was feeling didn't warm him all the way to his groin before he could turn back to the cameras.

He could feel the air in the room shift. He could feel the interest in the scene sharpen.

Your move, honey.

And, boy, did she move. Just as a TV crew arrived. *Brilliant.*

'Well, guys, I think it's safe to say that Señor Cruz has just shown us, in the most obvious way imaginable, that he's a big fan of Devine Design. You all know that I had the best of times this week—my clothes are for *real* women, with *real* bodies. I design beautiful, feminine clothes for beautiful, feminine women. And, hey, sometimes even a super-smooth dude like Mickey here can forget his manners, but we forgive him. He can't help it.'

She linked her arms through his and through Angelica's. Angelica was smiling as if her face would split, and for all the world he thought Ms Devine was going to take a bow. He couldn't help but chuckle at her little speech. He'd obviously upset her ego. Always the same—the brash types were the mushiest inside. So he'd give her this one, but he'd also make sure they moved well out of the range of any more cameras or reporters, just in case she got brave again.

'Angelica, I'm having the time of my life trying to keep up with all the highbrow conversation in the room. The car will be here in about five minutes. Does that give you enough time to do whatever it is you're hell-bent on doing?'

Angelica had stopped giggling with her little friend and was scanning the room.

'Yes, Michael. Of course.' She suddenly seemed a little tense. 'I'll just get you and Tara another drink—wait here.'

Another drink? With Whiplash? He moved to cut that right out of the plan but his sister was off, and it struck him, as it suddenly did at times, just how much she was like their mother in the line of her cheek and the fall of her hair down her back. Such regal quality and such ambassadorial skill. She smoothed and shushed where he bulldozed, and they both knew it. And it worked.

So what angle was she working now? Something was up.

'Where's Fern?'

He turned to Tara. She glared at him with those huge blue-black eyes. And then shrugged her shoulders.

'No idea.'

She lifted a glass of champagne from a passing waiter and knocked back a large gulp. Not quite the ladylike sips he was used to seeing in the women he dated.

'Thirsty?'

'Bored.' She pointedly looked away, then knocked back another mouthful.

'You should get out more.'

She turned to face him. Set a scowl across her face and pursed her plump, pouty lips into an even more furious moue. 'If it wasn't for the company I'd be having a wonderful time.'

'You would?' She was so easy to snare. He smiled as her scowl deepened. 'What's wrong with the company, then?'

'Isn't it obvious? I can't be the first person to call you on your appalling manners, surely?'

'Actually, my manners are the least of your problems.'

It wasn't like him to be anything other than courteous to women. His mother had been pretty lax about most things, but charm came cheap—the problem was this one got under his skin like a heat rash, and he didn't want to stop scratching.

'Meaning…?'

'You really have to ask?'

She swilled what was left of the golden liquid in the narrow flute, and then tossed it back in one mouthful. He watched her throat constrict as she swallowed, half expecting her to wipe the back of her hand across her mouth like a saloon whore from a fifties Western. Ms Devine was anything *but* ladylike. And she was getting all fired up—maybe this was going to turn into an interesting party after all.

'The only problem I can see is that you and your ego are still here. I can't be the only one who'd much rather you and your dull suit and boots got yourselves the hell out of here.'

Just as she hissed her little putdown another bunch of lovelies fluttered over. 'Actually, I'm not so sure everyone sees it that way...'

Far too young and, honestly, too far gone, but it was easy to let the charm drip as he kissed and complimented them. Tara stood to the side, pointedly looking away, then whipped out her phone. He watched her face change as her fingers scrolled the screen. She tucked it back in her little cube of a bag and seemed to brace herself. Interesting.

She walked over to him. Slowly. Almost dragging her heels.

'I'm going to get another drink—would you like one?'

He cocked an eyebrow. He hadn't been expecting that.

'What happened there? Did you get a text alert to be more pleasant?'

She smiled the fakest smile, but even though he knew she was forcing it, it was still a great smile. Her perfect mouth split to showcase white teeth that were perfect bar the front two, which sat at an offset angle to one another. Quirky. Cute.

'No, I just thought we should grab a drink to loosen up while we wait. But if you're too busy I quite understand.' She nodded to the girls.

'I'm loose enough, thanks—but don't let me stop you. I'm going to chase up my sister. Time we left the party to those who still feel the need.'

'Oh, come on. Just a little one? I'm sure Angelica will only be another minute.'

'I'm sure she will too. But I think I've indulged her long enough.'

'You see this as indulgence? People sharing some

fun together?' She swung out her arm, indicating the groups of people chatting, laughing, drinking, dancing.

He'd seen so many similar scenes in so many corners of the globe. At one time in his life this *was* his life. But party fatigue had set in some years ago and the whole scene now left him cold.

'It's all relative. Fun for you and fun for me? Not compatible.'

'You think? I bet we could find at least one thing we both enjoy.'

He turned back from the throbbing crowd to face her. Let his eyes drag slowly over that intriguing face. Was she coming on to him—after being so hostile? Did she have a short-term memory problem or a personality disorder to add to the mix?

'What did you have in mind?'

On anyone else the slight colour that crept over her skin would have suggested a flush of shame, but on her it was lost in the assault to the senses of hair, make-up, outfit and attitude. She was like a caricature. But she had something. He couldn't put his finger on it—yet. Maybe it *was* just attitude, or energy. Or overt sensuality. But he'd met a lot of women, for sure, and she did not fit neatly into any of his boxes. That didn't mean that he wanted to hang out with her at this or any other party, but it might explain why Angelica had decided to add her to her Pandora's box of friends.

'What do I have in mind? It's way too early in the night for me to tie myself down to anything specific.'

He grinned at her. Couldn't help it. 'You've got an answer for everything, Ms Devine.'

She grinned back, and this time it was natural. Like the sun coming out. Like there might be a natural beauty under all that make-up. *That* he'd like to see. But he was not going there. Yep, he was single, and until Fern was sorted—probably after Fern was sorted—single he'd stay. He could see no reason not to be. The only thing to be gained from adding emotion to sex was that it helped women to loosen up.

Even when they knew in triplicate that he'd had elective emotional bypass surgery, they still thought that they'd be The One to reverse the procedure. Shame they couldn't tune in to the notion that he liked himself better that way. No lies. No doubt. No guilt. Just sex. As and when he wanted. But not tonight. There was something about this one that lit up the warning signs in his head. And he was not in the business of ignoring warning signs. Not since he was sixteen.

'Sadly it's too late in the night for me to stay on and find out what you'll tie yourself down to. Or tie yourself up with. I'm going to get the car, and Angelica, and leave you to your fun.'

Though where his sister had got to was another problem. And one that was beginning to annoy him.

'Anyway, I'm sure Angelica will catch up with you later. It's been...interesting.'

He leant a hand on her shoulder and leaned down for the obligatory goodbye cheek-kiss. He could smell product—perfume, hairspray, cosmetics. He touched smooth skin. He felt the swell of her fabulous rack press against him. He let his lips linger for a second too long to be strictly platonic. His fingers closed more tightly over her shoulder and he curled his other arm round her waist, drawing her closer into him. He felt a strong urge to grab her by the bottom and scoop her against him. Her body was soft and nestled perfectly, and he moved his lips to her other cheek. But her lips were in the way, so he placed his kiss there. Just one.

She. Was. So. Hot.

Her eyes, when he stepped back, flew open. They were searching. Almost innocent. And again he got the feeling that she was a better actress than she got credit for. Still, it wasn't his business to stay and find out.

'Yes, it was…lovely to meet you.' She seemed out of breath and hitched back on her heels in a stumble.

He steadied her elbow.

'Don't you think we should wait here? I'm sure she won't be long.'

'No. Much as I'm tempted, I'm beginning to think there's something up. So—as I said—have fun, take care.'

He whipped out his phone and called for the car. Disappeared into the crowd, eyes on the alert. This night had tested his patience long enough.

CHAPTER TWO

IN A FEW seconds the party would begin to reconfigure itself. Blaring noise, pulsing lights, skin, smiles and wild-eyed stares.

What on earth had just happened there?

Tara reached out and gripped the table, her fingers closing round the sticky mess of spilt drinks. Michael's back was just disappearing into the crowd and she needed to go after him. But she was still reeling from that kiss—it hadn't even been a proper kiss, just a lip-press. But man alive, he'd aced it!

'Hey, Tara—you wan' a drink?'

Definitely—but she had work to do first. She needed to lasso Mr Wonderful and keep him occupied until she got the all-clear.

'Be back later, Jonny,' she murmured to her DJ friend, who had just packed up his vinyl. The same friend she had been texting like fury to make sure he hung around after his set—he was the best party animal she knew, but she was going to have to put him on ice for just a little while longer.

She checked her phone as she started the sticky trail through the club. Her foot connected with a shot glass and sent it spinning onto the dance floor—exactly what *she* should be doing.

Her phone buzzed. Another message.

Michael's waiting for you at the car. I've told him I'm on my way separately with a couple of friends. I'll drop Fern at mine first, then meet you at his place. Thanks so much for keeping my brother occupied. Hugs, Angelica.

Hugs? Who needed hugs? Fizz! Party! That was what she really wanted. But they were such nice women and—what the hell?—it wouldn't kill her to miss an hour or so. Actually, it might kill her—walking right into the lion's den without a stun gun. Guys who looked like that, kissed like that and, even worse, acted like that, were not part of her daily grind. She would need two layers of Kevlar at least.

The car would be out front. She'd have to pass another load of snappers—if they were bothering to stay up. She quickened her pace out onto the stairwell and tottered down carefully. The last thing she wanted was a jpeg of her landing in a heap at his feet.

But it was the slap of the pre-dawn grey-blue light and fresh air that hit her skin. That and the now familiar sight of a super-fit guy in a perfectly cut suit, lolling—yes, actually lolling—against a car that was… large and low and sleek. And he was killing the whole look—she had to hand it to him.

Michael looked at her. He raised one eyebrow. Opened the door and gestured her in. Now, that just riled her all over again. What was wrong with a few manners? She wasn't asking for anything more than a hello, or a please and thank you. He just couldn't seem to treat women as anything other than little pets to train and reward. But he was way off if he thought she would roll over like a puppy. After witnessing years of fear and subservience she had honed her bark and her bite to perfection.

'I'm not stalking you. I said I would come along to catch up with Angelica for a little while. OK?'

'You're invited. Happy to escort you.'

He was looking over her head—checking out who was watching.

'Embarrassed to be seen with me?'

He did a perfect mock gasp through his perfect teeth. Smirked. 'Now who's defensive?'

'Not defensive…' she said, bending into the car and knocking the top of her damn hair on the doorframe.

He slung himself inside after her and she scooted further along the seat. The backs of her thighs felt the cool of the leather, but the heat from his left leg where it sat open, relaxed and rock-hard, seeped right across the inch or so of space between them. She couldn't keep her eyes off it.

'Just perceptive.'

He cocked her a look, his arm stretched across the back of the seat and his hand just lying on his other thigh. The car started up and she noted other taxis and cars for a moment. Coming and going. And she was going further away from the club—her home away from home.

'You're perceiving too much, then. There's no sub-text—I'm out tonight to spend time with my sister. We don't see a lot of each other at the moment—she's mainly in London and I'm mainly in Barcelona, for Fern's school and business. So…'

He looked at her for a long moment and she nearly had to look away—his gaze was *that* intense.

'I'm here for them. Always.' Finally he drew his eyes from her and stared out of the window. 'But Angelica has her London circle, so it's all cool. She'll catch us up.'

He turned back round, actually shifted his leg up a bit on the seat until it was pressing against hers. She moved back, crossed her legs, stared straight ahead. He had turned that intense look back on her.

'No, I'm definitely not embarrassed to be seen with you.'

She flicked her eyes and couldn't help but twist him a little smile. She should know better, but he was a work of art. Maybe not her type—but undeniably attractive, and undeniably good at working women. Thank goodness she wasn't stupid enough to fall for him.

'That's such a relief.'

He laughed. 'You don't look relieved. You look uptight and anxious.'

She felt that—and worse. She'd had—what? Three glasses of champagne over three hours? At the party of the season? And now she was in what might as well have been a hearse, heading to a party for two that neither of them wanted to attend.

'I'll cope.'

'Sure you will. You're hard as nails. You can cope with anything.'

She spun round to see him watching her. Baiting her.

'Anything *you* could throw at me, that's for sure.'

His eyes lit up. His smile tilted and as the car sped along and the lights from outside brightened, then dimmed, then brightened, she saw his wicked, wicked mouth mock her. She saw it and she felt it. That same heavy tension she'd sensed twice around him now. She had to get a grip—it was beginning to feel as if her comfort zone was somewhere about two miles back. Where her immunity to men was second nature—normally.

'You're a very interesting person, Tara.'

It felt as if he had put his hand on her jaw, turned her to face him, but his hands were in plain view and it was some deep, feminine instinct that had her moulding herself to his will. Thankfully she was ruled by her head and not by her gut. Fortunately she could remember how to deal with very persuasive men…

She turned away, saw the back of the driver's head. Noted his eyes flick to hers in the mirror. He probably saw scenes like this every night of his life. What a shame she wasn't going to oblige this evening.

'So I'm told.'

'But I get the feeling you don't really know yourself yet.'

She felt her jaw tighten and her teeth clench. How arrogant.

'That patronising comment doesn't even deserve an answer.'

'But I'm pretty sure you'd like to give me one anyway.'

She shifted right round on her seat. He was watching her, smiling softly.

'What would you know about me at all?'

His eyes never left hers. Dark and demanding. She wanted to look away, but she couldn't, and that swell of fog or emotion or awareness bloomed around them again. She felt as if she was breathing in his air. As if something of herself was seeping into his space.

'Just what I say. You're a very interesting person but you don't fully know yourself yet…or you wouldn't be battling the attraction that clearly exists between us.'

'You must have some ego to think that every girl who rides in the back of your car wants to kiss you.'

He shrugged. 'I think *you* do.'

Still he stared, and still she stared back.

'Because you dropped one on me as you were leaving and I didn't slap your face? That doesn't mean I want to repeat it.'

'You *don't* want to repeat it?'

A low, quiet probe.

The car had stopped. She didn't know if they were at lights or at their destination. But nothing could drag her eyes away from his to check. A shadow was cast across his face, lighting only the mocking twist of his mouth. But his eyes flashed like polished coals in the darkness.

She swallowed. 'Not a chance.'

He was utterly still, completely and intensely present. She knew he could read her, but the chance of her admitting that? Zero. Even as she thought it the urge to feel his lips and taste his mouth swept over her. A shocking pleasure pulse throbbed between her legs. The air swirled thicker. She was definitely not in her comfort zone any more.

'Better get the party started, then.'

He broke it. Moved fluidly to the door handle. Stepped outside and held out a hand for her. She ignored it and gripped the doorframe instead. Stepped out and straightened in the lemony light of early dawn. The most sober, most disconcerted she had been at this time of day since…since she'd started realising that hedonism and ambition could be neatly packaged together. Since she'd purposely and deliberately burned every bridge that led her back to small-town, small-minded Ireland.

So what if her family looked down on her? She knew the truth. She knew she had a cast-iron marketing campaign that made her unpalatable to them and delicious to others.

She smoothed down her dress and touched her hand to the back of her hair. She dreaded to think what her face was like—lipstick probably smudged all over her mouth and the panda eyes slipping south. Who knew? That might be her best form of defence.

He was watching, waiting. Chivalrous, she supposed. A doorman stood sentry and a plush carpet swept ahead. The car behind them moved off and she had a sudden image of walking into this nineteenth-century apartment block with him, black suit, and her, white dress, as if she had done it a thousand times before.

Boy, she needed a drink.

She couldn't even look at him in the elevator. Didn't make small talk and didn't let the intense air-sharing affect her in any way. No way.

When the lift slowed to a stop she watched as the doors eased open and she stepped out and waited. He indicated left and she walked at his side as if he was showing her to a vault. He unlocked the door with a keypad and held it open for her. She took one step inside the room. Not as expected. No cherry floors, leather and chrome. There was smooth carpet, richly coloured rugs and silk-covered chaises.

She turned to comment and then she felt his presence behind her, heard the door click softly.

She bolted into the space as if branded, suddenly realising that her whole safety in numbers default was not going to be much cop here. How long were they likely to be here, alone, before Angelica showed up, with or without her little posse? This whole *keep him occupied* plan was all well and good in a nightclub. But claustrophobic empty spaces, even ones as grand as this, suddenly seemed to suck up her bravado.

'Champagne? Or would you like something stronger?'

He was moving into the open-plan lounge, jacket tossed onto the back of a posture-correcting couch. Even the furniture looked down on her. Devine girls sat on sofas with their dinner on trays and their eyes on the television. She could make out a dining alcove, with a huge dining table and artfully mismatched Deco chairs, complete with seat-pads in jewelled satins.

She definitely needed something stronger.

'What have you got?'

He swallowed his knowing chuckle and moved to a bar area. 'I'm sure I'll have what you want.'

'Mount Gay?' *Suck on that, smarty*, she thought, dredging up the name of the most inaccessible rum she could think of.

He produced it. Of course he did.

'With…?'

'Awww…' She breathed out with a slice of defeat. 'Just give me it on the rocks. I'll be gulping it anyway.'

He laughed then. 'You're surely not nervous?'

She laughed back, despite herself. 'What? You think a dragged-up fashion-head like me can't cut it in Luxe

Land? With European aristocracy like you and *les belles* Cruzes? You'd think I feel any self-doubt? No chance. I'll have what you're having, baby. Every time.'

'*Every* time?'

He snared her gaze. Held it. *Again*. Walked towards her with the glass of rum, ice clinking gently off the sides. Soft smile so sexy on that mouth, so sinful.

'Cut it out.'

He held the glass as he passed it to her, still smiling, cocked an eyebrow in question. 'What?'

'You know what.'

He stood almost in her space, with a matching drink, a roguish look.

'Do I?'

'You're freaking me out. You're just freaking me *right* out!'

He laughed properly then—no artifice or charm. Just a belly laugh. And suddenly she felt relaxed.

'No one could accuse you of not speaking your mind, Tara. It's refreshing, I have to say.'

She nudged her glass against his. 'You too. I suppose.' She took a long drink with the cubes bashing off her teeth and shook her head in wonder at her own self and this crazy situation. She could have happily strangled this man a few hours earlier, but now it seemed… it seemed he was maybe human after all.

'You got any music?'

'Sure. Come and choose what you'd like.'

She wandered behind him, watching his fluid, masculine movements. There was a man who worked out. No doubt. His ass was absolutely perfect. If she'd been in the club she might even have grabbed it, given it a little squeeze. She'd done worse!

He passed her his laptop and she flipped through a few lists. Taste was OK. Could do with a little education, but passable. She selected something mainstream, safe, stood back and felt the bass tones fill the space. That was better…

Michael. She turned. He was frowning at his phone. Then he placed it down on the bar and caught her up in another of those stares. What the hell was going on? Demanding dark eyes drilled straight into hers and made her feel exposed, on fire, exhilarated, choked.

'Everything OK?'

He nodded as he walked towards her. 'Fine. Just no word yet from Angelica.' He tipped his glass. 'Refill?'

'Peachy.'

She followed him to the bar. Stood watching. Jiggled her hips in time to the Balearic beats. Felt sort of good. House parties had never been her thing, really. Especially tiny house parties. Big crowds, big music, big hangovers. Absolutely. But there was something sweet and soothing about watching him move about his home, pouring drinks and looking so hot.

'You here a lot?'

He shook his head as he screwed the top back on the rum bottle. 'Once, maybe twice a month. But that's only temporary. I plan to move back once Fern gets a place at university here.'

Tara opened her mouth. Closed it. Things were quiet and calm and maybe, just for once in her life, she should keep her opinion to herself. Not her business after all.

'Cheers,' he said, and tipped his glass against hers.

She tipped hers right back, avoided looking up at him. But it was as if he knew. How weird was that? He laughed.

'I'm not giving you my eyes again, mister. You do strange things with them.'

He laughed again. Put his glass down. Stepped a little closer to her. The atmosphere felt heavy.

He reached for her glass. She held it—held onto the cool, the solid, the known quantity.

'What things?'

'Things…'

Her voice trailed off, quietly. He closed his fingers round hers on the glass. Fire round ice. And then she limply let him put hers down too.

His hand cupped her cheek. His fingers trailed across her skin. She closed her eyes and quivered as if she had been holding back a tide. And then she gave in. The moment when she could have stopped it had passed.

He slipped his hand to the back of her neck and hauled her up to his body. She pushed her hands to his chest and felt the muscle she had imagined. His mouth found hers and she moaned deeply as he took her, moulding her lips and tasting. Taking his fill.

He stepped her backwards with him, his mouth still fixed on hers. The hand that had cupped her head now touched and traced a path across her collarbone.

'Your skin taunts me.'

It was all he said before he resumed his assault on her mouth. He trailed down her bare arm, slow, warm and necessary. She made her own trail up—neck to jaw. A scrape of stubble rubbed at her hands and the scent of woody citrus filled her head. His tongue probed and licked and she fought to keep up. His hands were now on her waist, feeling and learning her shape. She knew he was going to cup her heavy breasts and she longed for it.

'Touch me, please…' she said, his mouth swallowing her plea.

And he did. He filled his hands with the heavy weight of each breast and he gently massaged. His thumbs brushed over her nipples through the satin material of her dress, and then he rolled them into points of utter agony and pleasure.

He didn't ask her what she wanted. He just gave her what she needed.

He scooped her up and strode with her into—it had to be his bedroom. Dropped her to her feet and spun her round.

'Dress. Off.'

He was worse than rude but she sucked it up like nectar and began to push silk-covered buttons through loops, to unzip and shimmy her dress over her hips. Nothing in the world would stop her getting her fill of him—of those warm strong hands smoothing their way over her skin. Even as she stepped out of it he was working magic with his touch—leaving hot trails in the wake of his fingers.

'You are so damn hot.'

All he said as he took his hands and mouth from her for a moment. She grabbed at his shirt, fingers useless on the buttons. But he stilled her. Stepped back from her. Looked at her standing in a pool of cream silk satin, her nipples straining hard through the gauze of her bra and her knickers shielding the last of her secrets. She felt as if his look was licking the flames of hell across her skin.

It was a party she'd never been invited to before. And she wanted some.

Her eyes drank him in now. Nothing but pure, firm,

wide muscle across his chest. She ran her fingers; then her mouth across it, inhaling and tasting and licking. He pulled off his trousers and her mouth opened in wonder. His thick, long erection jutted out and she couldn't stop herself from dropping to her knees, wrapping her hand and then her mouth around him.

But he heaved her up by the arms and lifted her to the bed. Placed her down and pushed her back. Then his hands wrapped around her panties and he tugged them down and tossed them aside. She sat back on her elbows and watched his face. He took her ankles and opened her legs, then dipped his head and licked the hottest trail of fire up and over her.

She jerked up and he put his arm across her chest. His head shook.

'Not yet.'

He dipped his head again and lapped and suckled her mercilessly until she began to feel the fire inside her building and spreading. Burning and blooming through her lower body. She looked down, loving the sight of his dark head nestled between her thighs. His mouth tortured and the spasms built until she lost her mind and her orgasm rolled and crashed. She screamed with the release and then lay still, aftershocks jerking suddenly, gently, quietly.

But his mouth, laced with the taste of her, came down swiftly on her lips, kissing and tonguing and building the fire all over again. He grabbed at her wrists and tugged her up the bed. She followed, unhooked her bra and watched, fascinated, as he sheathed himself with a condom. She longed to feel him inside her—just longed for it.

He wasn't going fast enough and she moved to sit up.

'Just lie back, Tara. On your back.'

And she fell back to the bed to watch him. And his eyes held hers again as she felt him nudge her open and then slide deep, deep inside. She whimpered—like a puppy—and then moved with his rhythm. All the time his dark eyes sparked and held hers.

What had she been doing those other times? With men who'd needed a road map?

He loomed above her, wide strong shoulders and caramel skin melding with the warm waves of pleasure that were rolling with every hard thrust.

'This feel good, Tara?'

Those eyes drilled and held and the intensity built.

'Hmm, honey? Do you feel it now—the attraction?'

She didn't give a damn that he was proving his point. He could prove it to hell and back if it made her feel like this.

And she grabbed his head down to hers and kissed him quiet. He leaned forward and flipped her round so that she rode him. She tilted her hips and shifted her weight and still she stared into those eyes. Something else was building—something huge and powerful in her chest—and she felt a moment of fear or wonder.

Then he reached up and touched her mouth. And rocked her even as she rode him. And she knew nothing could be this good ever again with anyone else. Her next orgasm surged and rolled through her as he jerked and exploded deep inside. And all the time his eyes held hers and she felt the burning squeeze in her chest return. Too intense. Too strong.

She closed her eyes. Hung her head and calmed.

A moment passed—two at most—then he threw his arms back and blew out a breath. That would be the sign to hop off, then. She braced her arms on the bed and slid slowly off. He still felt big and thick inside her, and it felt so damn good. But reality was beginning to dawn along with the early autumn sunrise. They had just had sex. He hadn't looked at her, touched her or soothed her. He hadn't said a single word. She was just a lay.

Silence.

The window she passed was undressed and looked out onto all her favourite London landmarks. She paused for a moment, imprinting the view on her mind—all the shapes and colours of skyscape and roofline—bridges, towers, clocks and wheels. All with the flush of dawn behind.

He blew out another long breath. 'You'd better get dressed.'

'I am.' She cast a look round to where he was still lying. Michael Cruz—beautiful, arrogant, not her type at all.

'Don't sound sore. I only mean that Angelica and her friends are bound to be here in minute, and it would best if we were ready to welcome her to a party rather than a love-in.'

'I know what you meant. I said I'm going to get dressed. You don't mind if I have a little clean-up first, though, do you?'

She knew her tone was bitchy, but he was such a swine. That had to be the worst post-coital talk she'd ever experienced. And she'd walked right into it. What was she even *doing* here? A favour? To a girl she barely knew and her extremely cosmopolitan sister? And, OK, she felt a solidarity with them, was happy to help them get one over on yet another controlling man.

A controlling man with a legendary sexual reputation that she couldn't even begin to conjure up any immunity to.

Why had she let herself in for this? What had made her think that she had the emotional wherewithal to pull it off? She needed rules and boundaries. She couldn't dabble like this! She could flirt. She could most definitely tease. But she knew herself well enough to understand that she invested too much when she took it any further. She couldn't help it that the heart she wore on her sleeve was just really well covered up. And the camouflage of her comments would be all that he would know.

'Go right ahead. There's a bathroom—there.'

He flicked his hand and stood up and she tried hard not to be impressed by that body again, but the man was beyond fit. What a shame his personality was so rank.

She felt around on the cool tiles for the light, but he came up behind her, stretched in and flicked it on. 'Thanks,' she said, aiming to shut him out.

But he stepped inside and reached out for her. Her skin was rapidly cooling, and she craved the warmth of his body, but she held herself rigid in his arms. He draped a heavy golden arm across her chest and the contrast was striking. Her milky Celtic skin was the perfect foil to his smooth caramel body. And even with her full breasts and hips she still fitted neatly within his outline.

In some perverse way it pleased her—but in the way that counted it annoyed her that she had gone and done what every other idiotic woman with a pulse seemed also to want to do with him.

Her eyes fell to her treasured necklace. Her grandmother's ring strung on an old gold chain. The little bit of love she fingered every day. Her little bit of sanctuary and strength. She touched it now, waiting for him to leave her.

'Look, I need privacy if that's OK.'

He took the thick, snaky strands of her hair that had worked free and tucked them behind her ear. Trailed his finger under her chain questioningly. She said nothing.

'Sure,' he said, but he spun her round and cradled her face. Kissed her. Slow and sweet. 'Whatever you want.' He gave her one more kiss and then pulled back. Trailed his finger down her shoulder and her arm. 'Beautiful.'

She watched the door close behind him and made a face. They were all beautiful—every one of the ten thousand women he must have slept with. And she was number ten thousand and one. What kind of fool was she that she couldn't even resist him?

She looked at the mess that stared back from the mirror—everything wiped off or smudged. She looked like her mother—weak and worried. And she felt sick at that.

Michael must have used another shower, because he looked like an aftershave advert when she finally got herself out of the bathroom and along to where coffee seemed to be brewing.

'Still no sign?' she said, thinking that *surely* Angelica would be making an appearance soon.

He shook his head and sipped at the coffee. 'No. Change of plan, apparently. Coffee?'

She shook her head. Who drank caffeine at this time in the morning? She had already filed this night in the 'delete' folder and was going to ditch the party at Jonny's and head right back to her bed.

'So what was the change?'

He had his back to her and again she felt her eyes

drawn to examine the way he moved, the slide of his muscle under fabric.

'Seems like everybody had enough of a good time at the club and by the time she got to her apartment she just decided to stay there. I don't have any missed calls—do you?'

Tara's mind whirred. What the hell was the right thing to say here? Surely something had happened so that Angelica had never made it over? Something with Fern, perhaps?

'Dunno. I'll check in a minute. So...'

'So you can have coffee, but the car's waiting when you're ready.'

He was sitting on a bar stool, the morning paper flicked out and open on the honey wood work surface. He raised the irritatingly small espresso cup to his mouth and she had the overwhelming urge to smack it right out of his self-satisfied hand.

'For the record, Michael, I reckon I misjudged you. I thought you were merely arrogant. But now I see that I was way off. You managed to single-handedly spoil a night that I'd been looking forward to for weeks. You're beyond arrogant. You know that?'

'Interesting. *I* spoiled *your* night.' He spoke to his newspaper. 'So you'll be ready to go? I'll phone down to let the driver know you're on your way.'

Tara scooped up her bag. And what was left of her pride. Could not get out of there fast enough.

Her heels sank into and caught on the thick pile of the carpet as she made her way to the door. Hot sharp tears pushed against her eyes. How could she have let herself down so badly? What on earth had she been thinking, having sex with a guy like that? No amount of pleasure was worth being made to feel like a hooker—an unwelcome hooker at that. He had totally wiped out every post-orgasm happy hormone and nuked her self-esteem. And, worst of all, she had let him. She should have acted breezy—even if she didn't feel it. Should have climbed off and swung her bra over her head in celebration. She really shouldn't be allowing his dismissal of her to hurt her like this. She was Tara Devine. She didn't give a damn.

Except she did. She so did. And it was so, so sore.

But every day was a school day. After what she'd been through it had to be. And this was small stuff compared to some of her other life lessons. She just wished she'd been better prepared. That she could wear her heart anywhere other than her sleeve.

CHAPTER THREE

'I'M NOT BUYING it, Angelica. Where is she?'

Michael strode through the hallway of Angelica's chi-chi apartment, his scowl black and irritation bubbling.

'Good morning, Michael. So we're in one of those moods? What happened last night? I hope you weren't this rude to Tara—were you?'

Michael tracked Angelica with his eyes as she glided through the perfectly furnished space. And that wasn't a question he was prepared to answer either—no one's business but his.

He looked for evidence of…anything, but the place was immaculate. Though Angelica did look drawn, which was a pretty unusual occurrence. She busied herself in the kitchen.

'Don't put coffee on for me—I've had too much already.' He'd thrown it down his neck as he'd tried to force out flashbacks of Tara's shock at his comments to her.

It had been the night from hell and he knew he'd been manipulated—he just didn't know why. But one thing was certain: the idea of losing control to a woman did not sit well with him. And he'd come very close to that last night. Hadn't been able to stop himself from taking her. When was the last time he had shown such complete contempt for his own values? He hated that out of control feeling—it was too fresh in his mind, even though it was over twenty years now since he'd truly been in a tailspin.

'Where is our sister?'

'Oh, Michael—for heaven's sake, she's in her bed! She's been working all week and she's only young. Try to remember what it was like and give her a little rope. Hmmm?' Angelica flicked on the coffee-maker and swept about, producing crockery and cream.

The trouble was he remembered only too clearly what it was like to be young. Not the details, but enough to know that night was day, uppers balanced downers and sex was available everywhere. Enough to realise that it was a carefully choreographed disaster, directed by his management and enjoyed by his fans. And had he not had the cold shower of his mother's death it might have ended up for him the way it had for too many others.

So when Angelica suggested 'a little rope' he would be using it to tie Fernanda down until she was mature enough to cope with it. Different story if she'd been like Angelica—but she was too volatile still. And this interest in the fashion scene was a worry. One that had to be carefully watched. Starting now.

'Breakfast? Have you eaten?'

'No, thanks—nothing.'

He walked on into the apartment and up to the spare bedroom, knocked swiftly on the door, cocked an ear and entered. The smell of booze hit him square in the face. He walked to the sleeping mound and stood over her. She was zoned out. Totally. So she had hit a wall last night.

He moved to the window and pulled open the curtains. Then back to the bed.

'Morning, Fernanda.'

'She needs to sleep, Michael—leave her be.'

Angelica had come in and was fussing about, lifting clothes and folding them. The room looked like a thrift shop. There was a huge glass of water at the side of the bed and jewellery and clothes trailed everywhere.

'Is she wasted?'

'Michael, calm down—she's fine.'

Angelica's fluttering was beginning to annoy him. Fernanda was lying in a white trash coma—he had enough experience to know that—so why was anyone trying to tell him otherwise? This was how it started. This was how kids like Fern took the hand they'd been dealt and tossed it up in the air. She was sixteen years old—exactly the same age he had been when he had begun to run with the wrong crowds and then down the wrong roads. Too cocky to listen to any advice that hadn't been about how great he looked or how good he was in bed. And totally too stupid and too naïve to know he couldn't possibly be good in bed. This was how lives careered out of control—when there weren't adults around who really, truly cared.

And Angelica might think she was doing the right thing—like his mother had thought she was—but they were different people. Trusting, kind, good. Not like him. Not at all like him.

And he wasn't going to let history repeat itself. No chance.

'Get her up, Angelica. And then you can tell me what

the hell went on last night. You think I can't see through your scheme? You planted that little sex bomb with me to keep me out of the way, didn't you?'

'Oh, Michael, you weren't horrible to her, were you?'

'You've already asked me that. And it has nothing to do with you what I did or didn't do, or say, to Tara.' He was getting distracted and losing the whole point of why he was here. 'Just get Fern up—I'll be in the kitchen.'

He strode through to the gleaming, glossy kitchen. His head pounded with too much caffeine and too much grief. He'd been played for a fool by three women in one night and for the first time in years he felt that things were spinning off in directions he didn't like.

He took out his phone and stabbed in the code. He had the rest of the weekend and then a trip to Spain on Monday. Things to sort, zero sleep and a crushing series of flashbacks involving Tara Devine.

Tara Devine? What or where or how had that name figured with his? Twenty-four hours ago he'd been given Fern's itinerary and had agreed to accompany Angelica to Tara's show. Had reluctantly agreed. Had sat through an hour of torture, counting his blessings that he had nothing to do with any of this puerile drivel any more.

Eighteen hours later he was banging the same Ms Devine for all he was worth and not getting anything near his fill. Was that his problem? Sexual frustration? It had been a while since his last lover, and maybe Tara had just sparked something.

'You're up.' He watched Fern's cagey steps through the kitchen. She was walking as if she had broken glass in her brain. 'Headache? Or worse?'

She kept her head down. He couldn't see her face for her hair but she sat up on a bar stool with her phone in her hand, ignoring him. Her normally upright posture was folded in on itself and she looked pretty fragile in her short pyjamas and giant socks. That didn't stop her from texting continuously.

'Put the phone down, Fernanda.'

She clicked it off and turned it face-down, but still wouldn't look at him.

'Where were you last night?'

'I was out. At a party.'

'So why say you were going to stay home?'

She looked up at him. Pasty, shadowed. Confrontational. He'd never seen her like that before.

'Why do you think?'

'Answer my question—and not with one of your own.'

She scowled from the depths and muttered, 'Tara's right. You *are* a control freak.'

'I'm glad we've got that ironed out. Tara's opinion is really important to me.' He was that good a control freak that the words were coming out calm and slow.

'Fabulous! We can all have a chat about that in a moment or two. She's on her way over.'

If he'd had coffee in his mouth he would have spurted it. But he was smarter than to give anything more than a bemused look to Angelica, who had just joined them in the kitchen—breezily, as if this was like any regular Saturday morning and Tara Devine was any regular visitor.

'Lunch? I suppose it's time for lunch…we seem to have missed breakfast.'

The ridiculously flippant musings of his sister were interrupted by the doorbell. He looked at the others but they were playing their little game. So he went through to answer it.

If Tara hadn't been expecting to see him she hid it well. The super-bright smile, pink lips today, and a flick of her eyes as if he was so much rubbish on the street and she would sweep it away. She walked straight in.

'Michael.'

On down the hall and his eyes followed the swagger of her ass in a leather skirt that fitted her like a second skin. That skin—her skin—he'd never seen or felt anything like it. Dove-pale and down-soft. His eyes trailed her all the way until she reached the kitchen. He heard a whoop of welcome from his sisters, even from the pathologically hung-over Fernanda.

'So you'll come?'

Come where?

He entered the kitchen. Saw Tara approach Fern. Hugged her and was rewarded with a soft smile.

'I'd love to. But I have a lot on, so maybe best to leave it. Until all the other issues are sorted.'

What issues?

Angelica's performance was award-winning. Little light smile and duchess head-tilt.

'Of course…of course. We could diary some time in for after Paris. I worry about leaving it too long, though. I think these may be the only free days I have between now and next month.'

Tara was handed a cup of coffee and now stood next to Fern.

'It's going to be tough. When would you need to know?'

Need to know what?

'Oh, I just need to know so that I can pick you up before we fly—or if you need to make your own way. I can collect you from the airport.'

What? Had they all been handed a script before he came in?

'What's going on here? Where are you all going?' Michael demanded, barely able to keep a lid on his growing frustration.

They turned to him—two dark heads and one blonde. All big eyes and mouths in perfect Os.

'Barcelona. Tara has agreed to design my wedding dress and she's coming out to stay for… Well, we can sort out the exact details later.'

'Is that right? Tara, maybe you and I should have a talk.'

'About…?'

About the state of Fernanda. About the signals she was sending his impressionable sister. About the mind-blowing sex they'd shared less than six hours ago. Her coming to Barcelona was not an option. He wanted order, not chaos. He wanted Fern calm and back at school. He wanted to be able to think about Tara Devine in the past and not look at her in the present and want to rip her clothes off.

He *needed* control over his head and his body. And Tara Devine seemed to have this insane capacity to reduce him to knee-jerk reactions and bizarre emotions. Who the hell wanted *that* near them? She'd already made him question his self-control, his sense of guilt and his whole value system. This was not an option. *Could* not be an option.

His sisters seemed to have left the room. But it was more the fire in Tara's eyes than the absence of other people that alerted him. As the door clicked shut she turned on him.

'I agree that we should talk. Me first. I came to your

house in good faith, expecting to catch up with the others. I told you clearly in the car that I didn't want to kiss you. I get in the door of the apartment and *you* clearly decide that no means yes.'

'Are you saying you didn't want to do what we did?'

'No.' She couldn't hold his eyes there. 'No, I'm not. All I'm saying is that the way you treated me afterwards was shocking.'

She turned back to face him. Her eyes were huge. The spill of vulnerable tears would have formed in any other woman's eyes but she was white-hot with hurt. And that hit harder.

'You sent out some pretty clear signals yourself. I came after you—in the bathroom, remember? But you wanted privacy.'

'Do you blame me? My pulse hadn't even settled back down and I was told the meter was running.'

'Tara, you're a player. Don't try to fool me that you were hoping for some gallantry. You know how these games work. You're in or you're out. And you were in up to your gorgeous neck.'

He looked right there, right then. Her silver slash-necked knit top showed more expanse of that silken skin. Her collarbone etched out a line that he had run his mouth over. The swell of her cleavage lay just out of eyesight, but the knowledge of it was all he needed to kick his lust awake again. He looked up and she was staring right back at him. Those blue eyes still stored hurt and the pinkest, plumpest lips still formed that tetchy moue. But she couldn't hide it any more than he could. They had a huge thing going on—a thing that he needed to rein in and redirect.

It had happened before—this kind of heat between

two people. OK, maybe not to the extent he was feeling it right now, but close enough that he knew how much havoc it could cause.

'A player? *Who* plays games with rules like the ones you made up? Rule One: act like an arrogant jerk. Rule Two: ignore the other person's clear warning off. Rule Three: muscle in like an uncaged beast…'

'Rule Four: respond like the Miss Whiplash you paint yourself as.'

She gave a little gasp there.

'Well? Did I call it wrong? You're playing with the big boys now, Tara. Better make sure you've thought it all through, because this isn't a rehearsal.'

She put her hands on her hips and squared right up to him. Her chest was heaving and her skin had flushed to the colour she'd bloomed when he'd made love to her. She was magnificent in her rage.

'Just listen to yourself. You absolute ego trip. I wouldn't *play* with you again if my life depended on it.'

'Your life will depend on you staying away from my sisters. So why don't you go and tell Angelica you've changed your mind?'

'Are you *threatening* me? Are you *seriously* threatening me?'

No, of course he wasn't threatening her. It had just come out like that. He needed her away—from them and mostly from him, and *now*. Because the way she looked right now, with her eyes flashing and her mouth open and moist, with her hands on her hips and her breasts pressing their tempting outline against the thin, soft fabric of her sweater, he wanted her as up close and personal as he could possibly get her.

'This isn't going to work, Tara.'

'This is going to work perfectly. And here's how. I won the commission for Angelica's dress fair and square. I need to spend time with her to get her thoughts. We've arranged that for next week. The fact that you and I had sex is irrelevant. The biggest problem is your need to control every aspect of everyone's life—including mine! Well, that just isn't happening. OK?'

She moved toward him to emphasise her little rant and it was all he needed. He reached out and cupped her face, stepped closer and hauled her right up against him. He took that pink mouth and made it his. He tasted her lips, her tongue, and silenced her but for the bone-deep sigh she finally eased out.

He moved her steadily backwards until her back was against the door. He pressed her with his body and ran his hands over her breasts, under her sweater and inside her bra. She yelped into his mouth with pleasure and he swallowed her sounds. Her hands were all over him, clutching at his butt, running over his shoulders, down his pecs and finally cupping his erection. She was hotter than the Mojave and she matched him in every way.

He stepped back, braced his arms on her shoulders, drew breath. She was right, of course. Even if she really was the full-on party girl she painted herself to be, and he was beginning to suspect it was a media myth, he *had* been bang out of line. But that was really beside the point. His first loyalty was to his family; and always would be. And no amount of sexual attraction or the spur of smart-mouthed comments were going to make her the sort of person he wanted hanging around. One week in her company and look what had happened to Fern. One week in her company and who knew what would happen to him?

'I don't need this kind of thing in my life. I don't want Fernanda any more influenced by your world than she already is. You've got your commission with Angelica—fine. But the rest is off-limits.'

The venom was back.

She recovered quickly and stepped to the side. One hand on the door handle, the other patting her hair. She eyed him, shaking her head and breathing her contempt.

'As I said. I make up my own rules. Deal with it.'

CHAPTER FOUR

THE LAST THING she needed was hassle. Of any description. The stress of organising the next show was off the charts and, yes, she was brazening it out in front of her team, but her shoulders were only so broad and her skin was only so thick.

She clicked the phone off and looked at it in her hand. Closed varnish-chipped fingers over it and wondered if it would ever ease up. So Dutch Ronnie was backing out. She should have seen it coming. He was too good to be true. Well, apart from how self-obsessed and downright dull he was. Beautiful, bisexual and boring. And also broke, it now seemed.

She rolled her eyes. This would mean another grovelling interview with the bank to extend her borrowing. And, sure, there were definite advantages to looking bad girl gone worse, but when it came to meetings with the suits that held all the cards she sometimes wished she owned even one thing knee-length in navy. The business side of life just seemed to roll much more easily when you played with a conservative ball.

Still, her media strategy had held her in good stead up until now. They loved that she was a natural at self-promotion. They loved that she 'was her brand'. And she knew most of them could see past her party persona when they focused on what was coming out of her mouth rather than what she was barely wearing.

That was the real irony, of course. That these stuffed shirts knew her better than most of her friends and *all* of her family. Funny that she could feel quite comfortable baring her soul to them, plotting out her five-year plan and being totally overt about how she wanted… okay, *needed* to have achieved a foothold in Europe within the next twelve months. The only thing they didn't know was why.

Why was she so driven? What had turned the quiet, unassuming mousy-haired, Girl Least Likely to Succeed into the competitive, controlling, crazy woman she was today? Did she even know herself?

Sometimes. And it didn't make her heart sing.

Which was why a head full of business was way better than any amount of navel-gazing. She just had to get things back on track.

Still, a week ago she would never have called this one! Angelica Cruz's wedding dress. It wasn't going to save her whole empire, but it could lead to some very lucrative long-term interest. If only she could keep her mouth shut and her gaze away from the eye candy that she seemed to want to gorge on.

She cast her eyes down over Barcelona outfit number one—a little red full-skirted silk-satin shirt-dress, peep-toe nude patent slingback wedges and… She lifted out what jewellery she'd brought, which was a joke: a few hoops of gold… She hated that she'd had to rush to pack like that. She back-combed her hair and then smoothed it into a ponytail. Red matte lips—no trace on her teeth—and…she looked down…yep, flaky nail varnish.

But she'd have to get around to that later. For now it was time to soak up the Cruz family atmosphere and start to tune in to Angelica's muse. A couple of hours of wandering around the house and gardens before lunch and then some time together reviewing the albums of previous Cruz brides that had been left out in her room on arrival.

And what an arrival it had been. Radio silence had been observed since she'd told Michael to 'deal with it' and he'd obviously gone all alpha and cracked his Daddy Cruz whip. Fern's pouting lip was big enough to trip her up and Angelica's almost brittle brightness had taken hold since they'd landed at BCN. Tara knew family dynamics well—Devine style. No words left unsaid, no look left undelivered. Tears, screams and tantrums. Then repeat until exhausted.

Until Grandpa Devine came home. Then everyone scuttled to the shadows. Whispers and eyes cast down. Favourite dinners and nothing a problem.

She picked more polish off, scraping her cuticles, drawing blood, feeling nothing. No, nothing was a problem—even in-your-face bullies like her grandfather. Her problem was that she'd had the front to call him on it. That had made *her* the problem.

So when the time had come to make choices—when some had got jobs, some had chosen college—she'd chosen the fastest train out of town. And never looked back. And, really, Michael Cruz was just a Hollywood version of Grandpa Devine. Smoother edges and whiter teeth, but that arrogance, that expectation that all females would do exactly as they were told…

She looked at the little pile of scarlet shards now lying on the crisp white bedcovers. *Sweep up the damage and get on with it. Get on with life. Because no one was ever going to stand behind you, let alone agree with you that women were created equal! Oh, no. Not your aunts, not your grandfather, and certainly not your mother.*

And that was why it was a far better idea to be completely and utterly independent. In every aspect of life. To stay as far away from people who would control her. And, if she absolutely had to date, she dated carefully—no lies, but no promises. And absolutely no men who judged her or disrespected her. They had to be totally in tune with their feminine sides. Or they didn't even get past first base.

And that did *not* make her a player! Damn Michael Cruz and his insults. Look what happened when she ignored her own rules…

The heat of the day was OK and the light was fresh and clear. Her heels clicked pleasingly on the marble as she walked through the house. The vibe of the place was strange—she couldn't quite tune in to it. There was happiness and love, but there was so much order, even with all the feminine touches that were so obvious—the flowers, the scents, the pretty soft furnishings and drapes. But among all of that was the *maleness* of the place—the presence of Michael. It was enough to suffocate the living daylights out of her.

She looked around. Heard voices. A voice. Followed the sound.

There it was again—just when she had filled her head with all the reasons why Michael Cruz was a flaw in the fabric of life she saw him, and life seemed to be a palette of beautiful colours.

Dark jeans literally hugged the best butt she could remember seeing on a man. *Ever.* The cut was fabulous and suited the length of his legs, easily thirty-four inches of hard muscle The simple white shirt didn't fool her for a moment—exquisite collar and cuffs and perfectly tailored to show off those shoulders—those shoulderblades. Hands should mould them and slide over them to absorb the breadth of bone and muscle. Fingers should feel the bulge of bicep and tricep.

Flashes of those arms holding her hips as she rode him exploded in front of her and she felt her legs almost buckle. She reached out to the edge of a chaise as he turned to face her.

The missile of that brown-eyed gaze hit her hard. But she held it until he flashed a look all over her, still talking in fast, low Catalan, and finally acknowledged her with a nod. She touched her hand to her ponytail—ran the tip of it round her finger and moved into the room, as if it was *her* air to suck and *her* view to savour.

Phone call over. A pause. The tension arced.

'Hi.'

'Hi.' She gave him a little grudging smile—all he deserved. 'Business call? Did I interrupt?'

He made a face that told her nothing. 'You get settled in OK?'

'Yes. Thanks.'

She moved through the corridor of space slowly, dragged the fingers of each hand across the veneer of a table, over the tips of tall cushions poking up from the back of a couch. Settled herself at the high, wide window, looking out for more life to absorb her than the all-consuming presence of this man.

'You look lovely. Your dress is very flattering.'

What? A compliment? She curled her lip and waited, for the *but*…

'You suit the colour too.'

She twirled her ponytail, looked out of the window. You couldn't call this guy. *Really.* She was all set to deflect and fire back and then out of nowhere a curve ball. Was that a strategy guys like him used? To double-disarm by being so unpredictable?

'Do you like what you see?'

She turned. Did he know she'd been checking him out when she came in to the room? Or was this another of his little control games? Didn't he know the rules? He criticised and she responded. Simple. *Compliments?* After their last little exchange that was just too weird. That smacked of mind games.

'Look, Michael, I appreciate the compliment, but I for one am a bit puffed out with the whole split personality thing you've got going on here. I mean, was it a different Michael Cruz who basically warned me off coming here? Am I supposed to predict if you're in a let's party mood or a back-off mood? Am I? 'Cos I haven't got the time to second-guess you. All I want to do is my job. And then get back to my world.'

She just couldn't afford to let her head get messed up by him. It was hard enough keeping the sexual attraction she had for him in some dark corner of her mind. The last thing she needed was to let him get in any more of her headspace. That way led to disaster. She needed total concentration for her business. That was her lifeline, her safety net—whatever you wanted to call it. It was the reason, ever since she'd left home, that she hadn't gone mad. So, yes, she *had* let herself go there with him—but she'd tried to set out clear rules. Mutual disrespect and a mutual, though waning, sexual attraction. Then back to business. End of. Surely he understood that?

'That's what we both want, Tara. I'm just being civilised about it. You're here in my home and I'm extending you the same courtesy I would extend to any guest.'

His voice was low. It was calm. It was laced with something she didn't understand.

'Oh.'

'Oh,' he repeated.

He was so sure of himself.

'So I should tell you that lunch is being served on the terrace.'

She cocked her head to look out there. Dishes were being set out and she did feel hungry.

'Shall we?'

She plastered on her best glacial smile and moved towards him. 'We shall.'

She passed him where he stood. She was so aware of him—the energy, the mind, the look of him. He watched her, and then all he did was put his hand out—touch the small of her back—and instantly a huge sexual high pulsed through her.

It was immense, the throb of pleasure unmistakable, and she paused for a moment, stifled a gasp. Stifled it for all she was worth because there was no way she was letting him see how he affected her.

She felt him at her back all the way through the house to the terrace. She moved like clockwork and kept her eye on the table like a homing device. Bowls of salad, meat, bread, olives—all the stuff she liked. Glasses. Thank goodness she could have a glass of white to take the edge off. She was feeling the edges right now—sharp and dangerous.

'Are the others joining us?'

She needed the answer to be a yes. Because couldn't he see that them being together, unsupervised, was going to lead them to the same place? Did he really want a repeat of what they'd started? She knew he wasn't just chipping away at her willpower—he had taken a sledgehammer to it. To the extent that now she was as likely to make a move on him as he was on her. And this was so, *so* not good news. She needed clarity and control. She needed her rules to work!

He was still behind her—tucking her into her seat like an overly attentive waiter. She scraped her chair in and out as soon as he had left it—OK, it was childish, and maybe a bit passive-aggressive, but he would get the point that she could move her own damn chair.

'Fernanda? No. She's going back to school tomorrow, so she's gone to the city and the library to get on with her assignments. Yes. Remarkably, it turns out she had *work* to do.'

'And Angelica?' She ignored his loaded comment and poured herself some sparkling water from a bottle with a spring-loaded cap. Waited for the reply he was forming as he did the same.

'She's popped over to Girona. Didn't she see you before she left?'

He flashed her a look as water splashed near the rim of his glass. Expertly twisted his wrist to stop the flow.

'No.' *So it was just the two of them.* 'When will she be back?'

He took a deliberately long time to answer—eased the cap back onto the bottle, placed it in the centre of the table, flicked out a linen napkin and sat back, glass in his hand, eyes on her face.

'That I don't know. She does her own thing.'

Tara struggled really hard not to get annoyed. 'Was it an emergency?' She could only assume that something important had taken her away without even so much as a *see you later.*

'If you can call a lunch date with girlfriends an emergency. And some might, I suppose.'

He was helping himself to food from the different plates. Sunglasses were removed from his top pocket and put on his face. He looked hot as hell. Mysterious as the devil.

'I'm finding that a bit odd.'

'Don't. Angelica is flighty. Someone will have sold her a line to get her over there—she'll be thinking she's on a mission of mercy. And she won't be worried about you.' He replaced a dish on the table, pushed it towards her in encouragement. 'You're in good hands.'

Which was exactly the problem.

She pulled dishes towards her. Scooped spoonfuls of salad and oily fish onto her plate. Kept her face down.

'So, have you been to this part of Spain before?'

'No.' Where was the wine? *Was* there any wine? She looked about. 'No, I haven't. I hear you have vineyards, though. That true?'

He looked at her. His eyes creased and his mouth split into that brilliant rarely seen smile.

'Wonderful vineyards, yes. I'm assuming that your interest in them means, in your very direct way, that you would like to have some wine? Which would you like to sample? *Tinto, rosado* or *blanco*?'

'Honestly? The way I'm feeling right now? If it's wet—it'll do.' She shook her head, pulled a face.

He laughed again. 'Come on, it's not that bad. You're in a beautiful place, gorgeous food—and the wine… Hey. Let me get you something special.'

'Special…ordinary. Wine is wine. You choose.'

He regarded her. 'Quite the enigma.'

'Yeah, you can explain that while I listen to the restful sound of a cork popping. C'mon, Michael—it's been a long weekend. And I could really do with a glass of your best Chateau Less Stress.'

'Wrong country, Tara. We're in Spain. Catalonia. You'll need to pay homage to the area before I can ease your tension.'

'Ease my tension? You *are* my tension!'

He laughed again. Not a throw-your-head-back belly laugh, but a rich, warm, easy laugh that instantly had her mirroring.

'I don't think you mean that as a compliment.'

He didn't know? He really didn't know that with everybody else she spent her day lining up the guns and then firing them. With him around she wasn't sure if she had even packed her ammo belt. Maybe he *was* oblivious? Maybe he thought she was this jaggy with everyone?

'Take it any way you like.'

He had so many dimensions himself. He never failed to amaze. Right now—when she should be feeling annoyed at being left high and dry in a strange country, while her business was effectively hitting the skids and the money to pay not only the wages of her team but the ongoing costs of the next show was trickling out of a Dutch Ronnie-sized hole in her piggy bank—right now she was smiling at the man who had riled her, stoked her, fired her to a crazy sexual high and then riled her all over again.

And it was, just for this moment, in the late September sunshine, the *best*.

'Tara, I don't want to be or even add to your tension, so why don't I just be your host for the afternoon, until Angelica gets back?'

'Why don't you be my host? Why do you even have to ask?' She picked up the still empty wine glass, looked at it pointedly and then raised it to her lips, sucking noisily on the air it held. 'Still empty. Come on, Michael, pour me a glass of wine and then let's get on with hating each other. At least we know where we are then.'

Hands on the table, he shook his head, still chuckling. Stood up and went to an ice bucket that had been sitting there the whole time. Pulled out a slippery, chilled green bottle and wiped it with a linen cloth.

'Hate is such a wasteful emotion, Tara. And it's miles away from what you and I feel for each other.'

She nudged her glass across the table and held the stem steady while he poured. The lemony golden liquid sloshed and coated the sides of the glass, but instead of instantly lifting it to her lips and downing a large gulp she stilled her hand, and her mind, and wondered what he really, *really* thought of her. She wouldn't give him the satisfaction of a second thought, but her own mind went there.

'I know I'm supposed to play coy at this point and say, *Why, Michael, what is it you and I really feel for each other?* But I'm quite sure I know what I feel for you. And at the end of the day—at the end of *my* day—that's all that matters.'

'Nobly delivered. But I couldn't be the age I am and have seen the things I've seen and not know that people's opinions are supremely important to someone like you, Tara.'

She felt the thin column of glass rotate between her fingers. She still didn't lift it to her lips.

'Maybe. But when I know the answer to the question what's the point in pretending I don't?'

She raised her eyes to him then. *Challenge.*

He sat opposite her again. Well back in his seat in that open-legged, confident way. Those probing dark eyes were trained on her in a way that made her want to lift up a shield. Or a spear.

'It's just a matter of time. As you move through life you'll find you care less and less about the opinions of those people who really don't matter.'

'And yours does?'

'With regard to our relationship? Sure.'

'Relationship? We don't *have* a relationship!'

He gave her an indulgent, absent-minded half-smile. Like an old uncle watching a toddler stumble over their first steps. Patronising, actually.

'Tara, any two people who have any interaction have a relationship. Of sorts. And we most definitely have had an interaction. A very memorable interaction.'

The shimmer of heat transferred from his words to her memory. A memory that was being etched more firmly with each passing moment. She refused to look up at him.

'The sex was OK. I hope the wine's better.'

She lifted her glass finally and took a long inhale, a

gulp, and then swirled it round her mouth. It burst on her tongue with flavours that she couldn't name and slid down her throat. But if he thought she was going to pay him a compliment after the way he'd treated her and spoken to her…

'Well? Is it?'

She put the glass down and lifted her lashes. He sat there like a king on his throne looking at an amusing subject about to subjugate herself. A self-assured smile played on his mouth as he lifted his own glass to his lips, waiting for her reply.

'It's passable. So, yes, better than the sex. Much.'

This time he did throw his head back and laugh. And she crashed out a laugh too. *Swine.*

'You should come with a health warning—an emotional health warning. Heaven help any man who doesn't have intact self-confidence taking you on. You'd annihilate him.'

There was something in that, she supposed. Maybe it came from her gene pool—though it would have had to skip a generation. Maybe it came from years of realising that it was easier to show strength than weakness? On any front. Attack—the best form of defence. Wasn't that what she'd learned that final time? Too many times hiding… So that when that moment had tipped, when she'd reared up and answered back—she would never forget how it had felt. Never forget that when bullies were actually confronted…the shock, the retreat…the world reconfigured.

'Yeah.'

'But I'm pretty secure, so I know you're lying through your cute little offset teeth.'

'That a fact?'

'You know it is. You know that we scaled the heights. And even before then—when we met in the club, in the car, in my lounge. Right here on this terrace. You can feel what I can feel. And I can see it all over you, even though you refuse to look up at me.'

She smiled into her wine glass. Too right. All of it. Every word he said. And then some. There was no mistaking the thrum of arousal in the air. Good to know he was feeling it too.

'Would there be any point?'

'In looking at me? Or in acknowledging it?'

She hazarded a very direct stare right at him. 'You don't hold any fear for me, Cruz.'

'That's interesting.'

She mentally raised her shield higher as he lengthened the look, seared her eyes.

'Though I'm not sure you're right there.'

She allowed him a smile for that. What did he know? What did he care?

'Whatever, Michael. Though, if we're on the subject of being honest with ourselves, maybe you could shed a little self-searching light on the fact that you seem to find me an "enigma" in private and a royal pain in the butt in public? Is that because I hold some kind of fear for *you*? Hmm? Worried that I'll act the way you seem to like me acting in private when your adoring public or, worse, your adoring sisters are around?'

Self-satisfaction. Not her usual tone, but he definitely deserved it. And he didn't like it. His brows knitted and his jaw tightened—which, if anything, made him look even more handsome, accentuated the square masculinity of his face.

'You deliver that as if it's a newsflash. Tara, but it's

obvious. You're… Of course I find you attractive. I also find you intriguing—genuinely intriguing. But the truth remains that what I find intriguing and what Fernanda needs to find in her life right now are two separate things.'

'I'm trying really hard to keep my wine in this glass and not throw it all over you. That's the second time you've insulted me like that. Do you *really* think I matter so little that you can assassinate my character because I'm here in your house on a commission? You think I'm so beholden to you that you can say what you like? Is this how you treat all your guests?'

'What I like is honesty. No games, no artifice or pretence. And I'm surprised that you are continuing to take offence instead of seeing things from Fernanda's point of view.'

She shouldn't be letting him push her buttons like this—she knew that—but she couldn't seem to stop herself while he sat there like the Commander in Chief, sipping his wine, chewing his olives. Just one more overbearing man, making all the rules. And wasn't that just the thing? The way they could twist it round to make you feel like the guilty party!

'Fernanda's point of view? You can't be trying to pretend that you care? What do you think her point of view would be if she found out that you were more than happy to have sex with me as long as no one found out about it? Maybe you should think about the level of hypocrisy you're exposing her to—never mind the fact that she might actually have found a job that excites her rather than a job counting your beans and boring herself to death!'

Maybe an olive had got stuck in his windpipe, because he sat immobile opposite her and it was as if a very black cloud had suddenly darkened the midday sky. She felt a strong urge to run indoors and get away from the storm that was sure to follow. But she didn't run away. She was not the type—not really. And—whatever he was about to launch across the table—it was only words. Not burglary or bankruptcy or any of the other things that either had already or potentially might have an impact on her life.

So she fought the urge to shy away from the intense mood that had descended and sat back. Lifted the glass now saved from being a projectile to her mouth and sipped on her wine, staring at him, challenging him.

'What's wrong? Suddenly realising that maybe you don't yet know yourself fully? Just like me? But it's OK for people to hurl words at you across a table or a car or a kitchen sink?'

'Actually, I think that right now you are more beautiful and sensual than any woman I have ever met.'

She was not expecting that. And even though it made her head rage it sent a dart of pure lust right to her core to know he thought of her like that.

She couldn't take her eyes off him. They roamed to his mouth, with its full, formed lips, and she remembered kissing them—the perfect fit of them round her own, the way he'd used his tongue and his teeth to stoke and nibble, the licks and thrusts that had matched how he filled her and how he'd moved inside her. She looked back to his eyes and this time the throb was something deeper, something more frightening than lust itself. It was openness, exposure, trust and care. And suddenly the shield was far away—out of reach, useless. And she was wide, wide open.

'But, whether you see me as a hypocrite or whether I see myself as protective, the issue that matters is that lust is just that. And if there's one thing I am sure about it's that I am more—and hopefully *you* are more—than a wild animal ruled by passion. So...'

She couldn't believe it—she was feeling as if her heart was beating on a plate beside her tapas, and he was talking as if he was giving a traffic update.

'So, regardless of how beautiful or sensual you are, this trip is about Angelica's wedding dress. Nothing more. I'll leave you to your own devices this afternoon. No stress. No tension. And no distraction. I hope you can deal with that.'

His chair was pushed back. He moved up onto his feet. Napkin tossed down. A smile. Little quirk of a smile. A final tug at the wine glass. Placed on the table. And he was off—away.

CHAPTER FIVE

BARCELONA OUTFIT NUMBER three. Two had been a swimming costume and wrap that Tara had shoved herself into when the excruciating silence in the house and the excruciating man of the house had both played mind games with what was left of her sanity. It made her feel almost like the unwanted child she'd once been—when she'd been too small to pick up on the undercurrents that little girls should be seen and not heard.

Well she'd more than made up for that since then.

She pulled out the dress and looked at it critically. A swirl of vibrant print on silk jersey. The obligatory deep-cut V. She held it up. Maybe a touch too deep? Had those words ever been formed into a sentence before? Tara shook her head—never in *her* mouth, they hadn't. But this was dinner with the Cruzes. No doubt in some ten-star restaurant that he'd managed to get a table at without booking a year in advance like lesser mortals.

She looked at her shoes. Great colour match but, again, nothing there was whispering *demure*. Everything was screaming *where's the party at*. Strange that she should be feeling like this tonight. It must be the knowledge that Angelica and Fern would be Princess-Grace-Perfect eating away at her self-confidence. But even that was unusual. She'd spent so long honing her own image—happily honing her own image and then reinventing it—that to question herself now was a bit odd.

She got dressed anyway. Maybe she should do something different with her hair? Less up, more down? Not straightened, but maybe waves? Big waves, of course, and a smoky eye, nude lip. She worked her way through the routine and then stood, faced herself in the antique mirror.

She was unrecognisable. It had to be the lack of eyeliner. She could have coloured in a path to Australia and back with the eyeliner she had used—but even her recent craze for the liquid line had died a sudden death. Must just be time for a new image—maybe something she could capitalise on in the next collection. She pulled a face. If she could capitalise on this she would be working a whole new demographic. Something was definitely off.

Her phone buzzed in her hand.

A text from Angelica.

Sorry, darling. Am caught up with poor Sophia. She has had terrible news and I can't leave her yet. Fernanda is on her way here too. Hope Michael is looking after you and see you very soon. Ax.

Great, just great.

She sat on the bed. Felt a bone-deep weariness. Sighed to her soul.

Another night of defending herself against his charm, his insults, his off-the-charts attractiveness. Another night when she'd have to screen every comment and field every probing, penetrative look. One to one, face to face. This was why she liked parties. To flirt and, yes, to hide. Because sometimes the whole effort involved in being Tara Devine was just too, too much.

She looked down at her nails. Now painted perfectly. Fingers bare of rings—because the only ring she wore was on the chain round her neck. Her grandmother's wedding ring. Her fingers absently found it and rubbed at it. Her grandmother had known what it was like. She'd had the battle scars. But she had protected her girls as best she could. She had put herself in the firing line and kept her flock out of his reach. But she was long gone. Long, long gone but never forgotten.

Tara felt the swell of sadness and crushed it back down. There would be no more tears. Not now. Not when she had come so far—so far away and so far on. So standing one more night with Michael Cruz shouldn't really be too difficult...?

Maybe she could try to make him see a bit more reason about Fernanda. Maybe she could do what her grandmother would have done—she would always do the right thing if it was going to help the underdog. All she had to do was remember she had her Kevlar body suit on under her dress. And not one single word that Michael Cruz fired at her would pierce it.

She snatched up a bullet-deflecting pink patent clutch and headed for the door. Time to dine.

The SkyBar? Or a backstreet Irish pub? Michael Cruz knew women. And he made decisions. So why was he over-thinking this simple decision as if it was a billion-dollar arms deal?

He glanced at Tara, sitting beside him in the car.

It was a deliberate act on his part to drive, and a last-minute decision after seeing her come towards him through the foyer. She literally took his breath away. Total remarketing job. But that didn't fit either. He really didn't see her as that type of game-player—the type that would try to read a guy and act and dress to suit. For one thing, she couldn't seem to hold her tongue in check for long enough to engage her control mechanisms.

She was a heart-on-her-sleeve blurter—a take-me-as-you-find-me or take-a-hike type of girl. If anything, she was a bit less ballsy than she made out—a bit more vulnerable. And he had caught a whiff of that vulnerability again tonight. She was preoccupied. Distracted? Maybe it was the enforced closeness they had again. Of course he could have left her to her own devices in the house—fed her and excused himself—but there was no budging Angelica from her latest project, and it was as clear as the water he was going to be drinking all night that Angelica knew he'd host, and he'd host well.

So where to take her? Yesterday it would have been the Irish pub without question—where she would have fitted in and had a laugh, and he would have relaxed, knowing she was knocking back shots and cracking jokes with the best of them. But tonight that seemed less and less like the right thing to do. She looked…she looked almost demure—if not elegant.

And quite why that was so unsettling him was anybody's guess. She was off-limits. They'd had their fun. And as soon as she had her meeting with Angelica and got the hell back to her world, the easier everyone's life would be.

SkyBar. Without a doubt. She'd love it.

* * *

She looked at him over the edge of the cocktail menu. Then dipped her eyes again. He ignored the city at night view that normally called to him and steadied his eyes on her.

She peeped up again. Then down. He laughed. 'What's wrong?'

Finally she closed the menu. 'How can I choose? I want them all! That's a ridiculous list of booze for a lush like me to cope with.'

'Why do you do that?'

She lifted up her water glass and poked at the lemon. Another of her little quirks. 'Do what?'

'Belittle yourself like that?'

She shrugged. Pouted. 'Depends what you see as belittling. I don't think that calling myself a lush is as bad as being called a bad influence.'

She pointedly looked at him and then sucked water noisily through her straw. A few people turned to look at her. She put the glass down with attitude, snaring a few more looks and responding with a confrontational grin.

'Ever get any paparazzi here?'

'Do you want some publicity?' He nodded to the waiter, who was expertly hovering, and ordered more water, a gin martini and a champagne cocktail. She could have whichever she liked.

'No, I just wondered. I am actually enjoying flying under the radar for a few days.'

She sat back in the seat and she did actually look as if the champagne cork that seemed to be permanently wedged in her solar plexus had finally popped and the fizz was trickling over her.

Now, *that* was a very stupid thing to think. His eyes

lingered where he knew they shouldn't as she twisted to take in more of the view. Her look tonight was all woman—with none of the comic book. She was lush, all right—but not in the way she'd made out.

Her thick, peachy golden hair framed the curves of her cheeks and lips. And her body was killing him. *He*'d been almost painfully sore since he'd seen her at lunch, and it didn't look like there was going to be any relief. Was it just that she had that perfect female ratio that tuned to some prehistoric part of his brain and made him want to throw her to the ground and claim her like a crazy man? Or was there something more complex? He wished he knew. And wished he could do something about it other than the obvious.

'Are you OK?' She was looking at him as if he was about to pass out.

'Sure.' He laughed. She had no idea—he hoped. 'How's your drink?'

She sipped on the cocktail and nodded appreciatively. Sipped again. Then again. Guzzled it. It was half gone.

'You maybe want to slow down. Remember you've got another one.'

'It's *so* good. Mmm.'

He had to look away. Her mouth was wrapped round that straw as if she was sucking up nectar. Her tongue jabbed the froth and his erection hardened. Maybe he should have taken her for a mojito on Passeig de Born. At least there would have been crowds there. And movement. Not the highly charged sex bomb that was about to go off right in front of him.

'So you're taking a break from publicity-seeking while you're here?'

She drained the last of the cocktail and sat back.

Her breasts rolled pleasingly under her dress and she crossed her legs. Was there any chance she was putting on a show for him?

'Not deliberately. I'm not in a place to do that right now—*especially* right now—but I can honestly say it's quite relaxing to think there's no need to choreograph the whole night just so I'll get the column inches I need. Though the way things are looking now I'll be back on the conveyer belt come Monday.'

'I didn't realise you were that dedicated. You must be exhausted. All that partying but one eye on the pay-back…or the fallout—because there has to have been some of that too?'

She ran her tongue over her lip. Chewed it a little. 'Always a risk. But, as I said, I'm not in the clear yet so I take every opportunity and make the most of it.'

'I thought you had things pretty well sewn up. Angelica mentioned your backers.'

She lifted her water glass and attacked the lemon again. 'They let me down. Today, actually. I just heard.'

She shook her head and a look of vulnerability slid over her. And it was striking. Those tiny flashes of the other side of her personality just added to the enigma. She sat quietly, stirring the shards of the lemon she'd massacred in her water. In a little world of her own. It made him realise how lonely she suddenly seemed. Fitted with what Angelica had confirmed on the phone earlier when he'd tried to probe a little more. That she was a master of self-created PR who'd honed the party girl persona—a single party girl. No one there at her elbow or her back. Maybe she had a great family—he didn't know and he didn't really want to know—but right now she looked as if she needed someone to scoop her up and take care of her. There must be someone close who cared? Women like her didn't come along every day. He'd certainly never met one.

'Don't you have other options? Other ways to raise the cash you need?'

Suddenly she brightened. Or at least she tried to brighten. The wide, full mouth split to reveal that unique smile and her eyes flashed. She raised the martini glass and threw the contents—almost the whole glass—down her throat. Wow, she could pull it back to the gutter when she wanted!

'Sure!' She spluttered, choked on the word, the alcohol clearly burning and making her eyes water. He reached over and patted and rubbed her back as she laughed and clutched her chest. 'Wow. That was strong!'

'Is it not a bit early to drink to the success of your new backers? Maybe let's get some food first?'

She was still choking and laughing and then, as he watched, it looked almost as if she was veering on the other side of humour.

'Hey, are you OK?'

Tears had definitely gathered in her eyes and the bursts of laughter were not sounding so funny any more. Was she...*crying*?

'Hey—Tara, *querida,* you're OK.'

He moved right over beside her. Curled her under his arm and tucked her head against his chest. Her hair was soft and he breathed in her scent for all of two seconds until he felt her push back against him and sit right up, her head still turned away.

'I'm fine.'

Her voice was still croaky but she was back in the game—no doubt about it. 'Do Not Touch' radiated off her in waves. Maybe she was one of those types that didn't like to be comforted. Though, thinking back, he couldn't say that he'd met any real resistance to his touch when she'd been naked in his bed. And he was back to *that* again. He really had to get a bit more perspective on this.

He studied the line of her back. No matter how she dressed herself up, Tara Devine was an ambitious, driven woman who just happened to push his sexual buttons like a pinball machine. She was upfront about who she was and what she wanted. Fine. But what she wanted was taking her in a direction he'd already been. And he had no wish to go back there—ever. And every wish to make sure his family didn't go there.

It wasn't a good world. It was shallow. It was dark. It brought out the worst in people. Had brought out the very worst in *him*. It wasn't the first time he had realised that with his mother's horrific death had come a very big silver lining in the form of a crushing sense of responsibility. It hadn't seemed that way at the time. But in a way it had been his saviour. Because he knew that in his day he had been much, much wilder than Tara Devine had *ever* been.

'You sure? Did it just go down the wrong way, or were you overcome with grief at finishing your martini? I can always get you another. You just need to ask. No big deal.'

She turned a blotchy face and gave a little half-smile. 'Thanks. All good. Maybe I'll have another water.'

'So. Backers. You need any help with that? Or you got it covered?'

'Nah, I'm going to be fine. There are plenty more Dutch Ronnies out there.' She settled herself back in her seat—at least she'd got whatever emotions had been rolling through her back under wraps.

'Dutch Ronnies? Is that a type of condom?'

She raised an eyebrow. 'Not one that I remember *you* using.'

He had to admit that his use of condoms that night was nowhere near as maxed out as he would have liked it to be. In fact, had he known then what he knew now, he would have planned a much, much better night. One where she didn't slip off and out of his grasp. One where he had the chance to bend her into the shapes he had spent a lot of time imagining since. Some of which had taken even *him* by surprise.

What was he getting himself into here? It was time to get back on track.

The waiter put down their water and they waited in silence until he left.

'Do you think Angelica will be back tomorrow?'

He had to admit that he was counting on it. 'Honestly? I don't know. I think so—but what you need to know about Angelica is that she manages to make everything fall into her lap. And she sometimes forgets that there are agendas other than hers. Not that she's selfish. Far from it; in fact most of what she's about is helping other people—finding what I call her "projects" and moving them on, like a little ambassadorial conveyor belt.'

She looked directly at him with eyes that were earnest and blue as truth. 'Does she see me as one of her projects?'

He could only answer as honestly as she deserved. 'Truthfully? I think so. But that's no reflection on you and no statement about your independence or capacity. She gets attracted to people for all sorts of reasons, and she gets as much out of helping people as they get from her help.'

She finally let his eyes go and the dip of lashes curled a shadow on her cheek. Golden light from the table candles danced across the planes and hollows of her face. She was bewitching. Too bewitching.

'I know. I'm not that naive. I'm just so used to being the only one batting for Team Devine I suppose I find it hard to understand the motivation of anyone who would want to help just for the sake of it.'

And just when he'd thought he had her all figured out… It wasn't just her words—her tone, just for a moment, had been so soft, vulnerable. And he felt again that sense of responsibility she stirred in him. She really must have had a raw deal somewhere along the line.

'Not everyone in business is cut-throat, Tara.'

'But most are.'

'Is that why you project such a ball-breaker image?'

She shrugged. 'I project who I am. I told you: I don't play games. It's just that some people deserve to have their balls broken. And others…' she slanted a flirty look right at him '…deserve to have their balls…'

He turned right round to face her. 'Are you seriously going to finish that sentence?'

She threw her head back and laughed. A laugh from her soul that washed through him like a fierce warm wave. And then he was really in trouble.

He reached for her. No way he couldn't. Took the back of her neck in his hand and pulled that mocking mouth right down. Crushed it. Over and over and over. He thrust his tongue in so deep that he stilled her and felt her go limp in his arms.

He held her close, then closer still, as he dragged her to him across the leather of the seat and pressed his body into hers, feeling every curved inch of flesh. Took both hands and cupped her jaw, still not letting her up for air, and kissed her more. Skimmed one hand over her collarbone and laid it flat against her chest, his fingers almost circling her throat.

And he felt her respond. Heard her respond. She liked that—oh, yes. He pulled his mouth back and stared deep into glazed eyes that had fluttered open. He searched her, shared the air that she was drawing in and out, and felt like the mad man he knew he was around her. She was so dangerous for him. Dangerous but irresistible. He *had* to have her again. Had to take it to the next level with her. Not intimacy, or love, or any of that romantic stuff. Just pure animal lust—because he recognised it in her.

She was tuned in to him so well that he was going to give her the best time of her life. And maybe then she wouldn't feel quite so all alone.

He stood up, threw some bills on the table and reached for her hand.

'Come on—we're going home.'

But she sat there. OK, she was still in a state—as was he, a very painful state—but she made no move, didn't even look up at him.

'No,' she said. 'No, Michael. It's not happening.'

He trailed his eyes right round the bar. He saw people laughing, people chilling at the aqua-lit pool. Waiters walking past, professionally oblivious. A party next to them of elegant middle-aged women who clearly recognised him. And then his gaze fell down to Tara. She sat there, golden head dipped. Arms stretched, holding on to the edge of the seat. Knees locked together.

'You don't want to do this? You don't think we have explosive chemistry?' Seriously, in his life he had never known such off-the-charts detonations when he'd just kissed someone.

'It doesn't matter about the chemistry. What matters most comes before and after the chemistry.'

He looked down at her. Kissing him like she was pouring her soul into his and then saying *thanks, but no thanks*?

'I didn't figure you for a tease, Tara.'

'But I figured *you* as an everyday player who wants to take a woman to bed—only if the important people don't see, of course—and then, once he's played, he tosses her back. He doesn't give a damn about how that makes her feel. And, Michael…' She looked right up at him and the fire was back. 'I am way better than that.'

She stood up.

'Just because you caught me in a vulnerable moment just now because some other guy let me down… this time over money, but, hey, who's counting? Just because I got a little stressed about it all. It doesn't mean I would ever, *ever* go back there with you. Why would I repeat anything that made me feel dirty and worthless?'

Sometimes he really did not understand women. 'I really hate to think that you felt dirty after what we did, Tara. We *do* have chemistry. You want to call it something else, go right ahead…'

'Chemistry doesn't give you the right to treat me like you did—and probably will again if I let you.'

Her eyes were glazed with tears but they flashed blue fire and her mouth shaped her anger. For the second time nothing could stop him. He took a fistful of her hair, twisted it and drew her fast and close to meet his mouth. One long, silencing kiss and one tug of his wrist to let her know her words were empty nonsense. And she buckled. At the knees.

He held her, turned his mouth to her ear and felt her shiver to her core. 'Say what you want. Act like you don't want it. But we both know this is happening again. And the next time you'll be begging. Screaming for it. And you won't feel dirty or worthless. You won't feel angry. You'll feel more alive than you've ever felt in your life. Understood?'

He scooped her under his arm and walked her to the elevators. She didn't fight him, but he knew he had winded and wounded her. If he'd made her feel any of those things then he'd more than make it up to her. Even though he knew, sure as he knew his own name, that she wasn't going to roll over and let him.

CHAPTER SIX

THERE WAS NO DOUBT that the beauty gene ran deep in the Cruz women. Tara flicked through pages of photographs, each one showcasing yet another even more sultry dark-eyed, dark-haired goddess. Photos from decades past of women—a few even in the traditional dark bridal colours, wearing mantillas and looking in some cases as if they were going to a funeral rather than a wedding. She could pick out clear family traits—the long, graceful neck and the high, wide brow. Open features, easy loveliness—and, more than anything, elegance and intelligence.

She glanced up at Michael, who was pouring coffee for them both and eyeing her carefully. And he had the male version of all of that in spades. *Damn him.*

She still hadn't got over the scene at the SkyBar. Him kissing her so publicly and then dragging her off like a caveman to the elevator. She'd more than put him straight when she'd got her breath back—and he'd more than backed off. Right to the corner of the elevator. And then he'd kept a respectful distance for the rest of the evening. Or at least pretended to. She still wasn't sure of him or his motives…

And she still didn't know how she'd got through it.

Emotions she hadn't felt for years had been on a rolling boil and she'd really struggled to keep a lid on it. Tears! *Why?* She hadn't even shed a tear in her darkest moments. She'd got her act together and got out. Never looked back. So why was it all bubbling up now? Just when she could see the light at the end of the tunnel—just when everything was stacking up in her favour. OK, *most* things… She could cope with the Dutch Ronnies of the world letting her down—all she had to do was hunt hard enough and another couple would roll along in the next limo.

But the intensity…

She flicked another glance up at Michael—he was still studying her on the quiet. The cut of his jaw was serious and he was definitely holding back. The intensity of this man was unravelling layer upon layer of stuff that she'd thought was buried for ever. It wasn't that he directly reminded her of her grandfather. It was more that she hadn't met anyone—not one single person—who made her stop and question herself, who made her wonder even for a second if what she was doing was completely and utterly correct.

Since she'd left home she'd known that what she was doing was on the money. Getting the courage to leave had been easy. Keeping the courage going had been easy. But suddenly, just when she could almost touch the prize, she felt she didn't even know if she had any right to claim it. He had unsettled her so much—made her feel so confused about herself. Had unleashed so many old ghosts that the urge to run was building higher and higher.

She was going to give Angelica until the end of the

day and then she was heading home. She had to. For her own sanity.

'See anything inspiring?'

She felt the now familiar rush and whoosh of adrenalin as Michael settled himself beside her on the floor, extending long legs in dark denim out in front of him.

Her knees were tucked to the side, wrapped in cute cropped trousers and low-heeled slingbacks. Between them lay the piles of photos and photo albums. He was a foot away, but still the energy zinged and it was as if his hands were touching her. She budged slightly over…away.

'Yes. So many traditional elements could be incorporated.' She turned more pages. 'It's just a pity Angelica isn't here to give her view.'

He sighed—and did he actually move another inch closer?

'Honestly? She can't be too much longer. I think this is a record. Usually she indulges for a few hours. A day—and a night—is pretty extreme stuff even for Angelica.' He leaned forward and started to sort through some albums. 'Have you got any of my mother?'

She hadn't wanted to say. Yes, her second wedding—to Angelica and Fernanda's father, a respectable Spanish politician—was there, and it was everything she had expected. She'd been a classic Spanish bride of her time. But the wedding album Tara had really wanted to see—the man who had won her nineteen-year-old heart, Michael's father—was missing.

She handed him the album she had and he quickly scanned it.

'You're not in any of them.'

The words were out before she could stop herself.

'No. I'm not. I wasn't there.'

He sounded matter-of-fact again. So she could probe?

'How old were you?'

He continued to flick pages. 'Not sure. Teens. Maybe seventeen. Sixteen?'

'And you weren't invited?'

He half laughed at that and a little tension bubble popped. 'I really don't remember.'

She turned to him and frowned. 'You don't remember? I don't buy that, Cruz.'

He shrugged and paused on a couple of pictures. 'It looks like it went well. Looks like it flowed exactly as my mother would have planned it. Which would have been like a military operation. And genuinely…' He looked right at her with the gaze that captured her every time. 'Genuinely, I don't remember if I was wanted there or not.'

'*Wanted* there? Are you serious? Why not?'

Who wouldn't remember whether they were invited to their own mother's wedding? Unless they were so spaced out at the time… Those were the rumours, of course. The pretty boy, the child star had gone out of control. With a mother who had been more interested in solving other people's problems than her own.

He and his girlfriend had been the sweetest little toxic twosome. He'd been the European face of the biggest soft drinks company in the world, and then he'd hit the skids. Oblivion. At least he'd made it out alive…

'Ah, it wasn't the best of times for me. Truthfully? She may have wanted me there, but I was in no fit state to know that, and if she didn't want me it would have been for the same reasons—that I'd let her down, turn up high or drunk or both. Probably bring some totally inappropriate girl or even a whole bunch of inappropriate girls. So it was for the best that the most important day of her life was spent *without* the carnage that I'd have created.'

He was speaking in that matter-of-fact way again. Tara didn't know if she would have been able to pull off nonchalance like it—ever. He seemed to major in it. But she couldn't see it from his mother's point of view. Surely any mother would want her own son to be at such an important event? Surely it wasn't all about appearances?

'Maybe your memory is clouded? Maybe your mother did want you there but you got caught up in…I don't know…stuff—the stuff you did?'

He shook his head and smiled at her indulgently. 'I'm not hurt, if that's what you're getting at. I was out of control. I was all about me—as selfish and hell-bent on a crazy cocktail of self-destruction and self-promotion as it was possible to be. Don't think that my mother hadn't tried to reach me—of course she had—but I was out. Out for the count.'

Tara knew the crazy cocktail he was referring to. Her own life could be said to currently resemble a 'lite' version of that. But only she knew that her self-destruction was more fiction than fact. His past, from what she had picked up on, was more of an Armageddon than any of the little sham-pagne celebrity after-parties that *she* tripped up at.

'She must have been out of her mind with worry about you.'

He pulled one of those impenetrable faces. Smiled at an image of his mother, standing with regal elegance oozing out of every pore of her perfectly postured body.

He trailed his finger round her face and nodded—a tiny nod.

'I'm not judging her. She had every right to get her life back on track after losing my dad like that. Then all the heartache of coming back to Spain and building bridges, re-establishing herself.'

Tara said nothing. Not sure if he wanted to keep talking. And not sure any more if she wanted to listen. It was all getting a bit too much like a therapy session. And she wasn't prepared to man up and go next.

'Any photos of that wedding—of your mum and dad?' She *desperately* wanted to see those. To see the young Maria Cruz before she became the *grande dame* of Spanish society. To see the man who had won her heart: Michael's father.

A mirthless laugh. 'It wasn't that kind of wedding. No white dress or morning suits. No bridesmaids catching the bouquet. Not a chance. It was an elopement—Spanish wealth and class meets London East End. A match made in heaven—ending in hell.'

Bittersweet desolation. It was there in his voice. His usual black and white, here-are-the-facts tone had darkened and she was sure there was still something very, very raw in there.

Tara fought an urge to reach out and touch him. He was so close. The sinew of his bronzed forearm bunched and stretched as he flicked through more albums—but there was no way he was really looking at the pictures. Still, she didn't probe, or reassure, or offer any kind of solace. But it was getting harder. He was getting easier.

He put down the albums, stretched out his legs, seemed to lean a little closer—but maybe that was just her imagination.

'They were your classic explosive relationship. Fire and passion, uprooted lives and lost friends and family. And all for what? A fantastic sex life and a baby?'

'You?' she asked.

He nodded. 'And then it all fell apart. He'd had enough. Or at least he said he'd had enough. He worked for some very well-connected people—and I don't mean the royal family. So, whether he was trying to protect her, and me, or whether he really had had enough of her…' He shrugged, tipped his head back onto the leather seat, stared into nothing. 'None of that really matters because she was shipped home, back to Papa, and ten days later he was dead.'

Tara felt a stabbing heat in her eyes. She reached for his arm. 'I'm sorry.' Her fingers closed over warm skin and muscle and she kneaded softly. He didn't budge. Didn't notice. Kept his head straight ahead and his eyes on who knew what? It was as if she wasn't even there.

Finally… 'Don't be. It's nothing to do with you. Barely anything to do with *me*. And it's well in the past. So there's no need for analysis or sympathy.' He turned then and his face was almost weary.

Her fingers stilled. He kept his eyes on her. And it came again—that huge swell of strange emotion—as if he could see right inside her and she could see right into him.

'The one thing I did take from it, though, is that no amount of passion is worth ripping your family apart for. Everything fizzles and dies. Family is what holds us together.'

Tara instantly retracted her hand. *Family is what holds us together.* The words rolled round her mind. He really thought that? Then he'd had a totally different experience than she. In her book, family was what drove people apart. Not one single member of the Devines from back home had ever called, written or visited. Not one. For all she knew they could all be dead and buried.

'So what about *your* family? You never really mention them.'

She simply stared. How could she begin to tell him about that lot? Where to even start? *Oh, I had a wonderful grandmother, who was a victim of domestic abuse by her husband until she died. And she bore it like Joan of Arc. And instead of being taken to task for his outrageous behaviour he was left to fester and get worse. Everyone ignored it. Everyone excused him. No one wanted to know. And no one was safe, not even children. And all the while her mother, with her own crucifyingly low self-esteem sat back and let him.*

Heaven help her if she ever asked about her father. That was tantamount to war crime. All in all, they were a perfect family. You couldn't make it up.

'Tara?'

'My family?'

'Yes. Your family? Got any? You know—brothers? Sisters? Skeletons in your closet?'

She just couldn't form the words. Her eyes continued to be held by his but her lips wouldn't shape any words. What words *were* there? No way she was going to start offloading any of *that* drama to anyone. Least of all Michael Cruz.

'You OK?'

He had shifted right round to face her now. His elbow rested on one leg, bent at the knee, his other arm lay along the leather cushions. His inscrutable face was showing interest. And she wished to hell it wasn't.

He reached out for the hand she'd placed on his arm. But she jerked it up and away.

'Fine. Of course I'm fine. Why wouldn't I be fine? I really, *really* need to get some ideas down for Angelica. Can I scan these? On the copier in the office? I think I've got all I need here now.'

She tried to stand. He looked up at her. His interest was getting more piqued. She was stepping on the photos. Low kitten heels pierced an album cover. He looked at them. Back up at her.

'Calm down, Tara, I'm only asking. It's no big deal if you don't want to talk about them.'

'What's there to talk about? No big deal is right.'

She bent to catch up the loose photos that had fallen out of albums. Stood and dropped another load on the floor. He was on his feet in a heartbeat.

'I've got them. It's OK.'

She hated that he was fussing over her. Hated that she was making such a fool of herself. He'd only asked her a simple question and she was behaving like a complete lunatic.

'I'm fine! I'm absolutely fine… Look. Really. This is going to be better if I get these pictures copied and work on them back in London. I think I'll change my flight and leave in the next few hours. No, you don't need to drive, get a driver…I'm cool with it.'

'You're cool with what, exactly?'

He was lifting the photos out of her arms. He laid them down on the table next to the leather couch. Slowly. Carefully. Put his hands on her shoulders and stepped her back, steered her round. Gently pushed her down onto the couch. Eyes on hers the whole time.

'What do you think you're doing? You know I hate that macho act you shove at me.'

Instead of lifting his hands away he massaged her shoulders. Tiny little circles but pretty near perfect touch.

'This isn't macho.' He kept kneading. 'This is what you need right now.'

She opened her mouth and he *actually* put a finger on it, shushing her. And then he laughed at her shock.

'Tara, *querida*, you need to learn to relax. Stop being so defensive. I only want to help you. Live in the moment and go with the flow.'

'What? Are you a Buddhist now?'

He smiled softly. Moved his hands from her shoulders to cup her jaw. Thumbs traced cheekbones. Slowly. And she felt as if she could feel every line of his finger, every pore, as he swept his soothing path. She sat where she'd been placed and drank in his comfort. And for a moment it felt like heaven. Warm and welcoming. Easy and soothing. For that moment she felt she didn't need to keep fighting. That she didn't need to hold up her shield and her sword and run at everything.

She felt her shoulders sag and her heart slow. Felt her breathing deepen and steady.

The thumbs trailed down her cheeks. He dragged one firm pad to her mouth. Round the edge of her top lip and down over the swell of her bottom lip. Velvet brown eyes bored into hers. Her lips opened. Her tongue eased out and tasted his thumb, welcomed it inside her hot, wet mouth. She suckled it as she stared at him—not even knowing herself. Not knowing that she was the kind of girl who would do that. But it felt so special and so simple. Felt so right.

'Tara.'

He said nothing more. Lifted his hands back and placed his mouth to hers. The softest, gentlest kiss she could ever imagine. Barely a kiss. Her eyes flew open and he opened his slowly too. Long moments passed. He cradled her face again, ran thumbs in gentle circles over her cheeks. Looked long and steadily into her eyes.

'Give yourself over to this. Just for now.'

And he dipped his head again and kissed her with such kindness and care. She felt something building inside her and it frightened her. She tried for a moment to pull back but he steadied her.

'No, no, no. Just a kiss. Nothing more. Just a kiss.'

She felt his lips on hers once more, this time firmer, reassuringly firm, and then his tongue opened a path inside her mouth and she knew this was the best kiss she had ever had. His mouth was the perfect foil for hers; his tongue already knew her mouth and stroked the hot, wet corners. His warm breath mingled with her own.

Wave upon wave of pleasure began to wash over her. Her body loved what he did and swelled up, opened like a flower for him. A sound built in her throat. A moan of abandonment and joy. She placed her hands over his and then moved them to his face. Felt the harsh trail of stubble and loved it.

She tried to deepen the kiss, tried to get him to move to a higher gear, but he resisted. He pulled his face back, out of reach, and she saw how greedy she was for him. Her tongue followed in the wake of his mouth and he smiled.

'You feeling better? Calmer?' His hands held her back at arm's length.

She swallowed back her hunger. Gulped down her

craving. Eyes drank in his stepping back—and she felt the distance choking. Why had he stopped? Why pull away like that? Was he regretting what he'd just done? Again?

'Calmer?' *Did* she feel calmer? No. She felt open and vulnerable, and those were two emotions that she hated feeling. 'Thanks, but I think I'd feel more calm if you left me alone.'

He chuckled at her. Shook his head.

'Tara, don't start going all defensive again. You and I are hot together. And you should use that to your advantage—take pleasure from it. That's all.'

'Hot but inappropriate? Just like the girls you never took to your own mother's wedding?'

He took her verbal missile, held it and crushed it right in front of her. He reached out and trailed a finger down her cheek. She flinched. Not because he'd caused her to, but because she wanted to. She would show him rejection right back.

'Tara—you're harder on yourself than anyone I've ever met. Why is that?'

She forced her eyes shut rather than look at him. Couldn't bear the fierce rush of tears that threatened. Could feel the cauldron of emotions bubbling up again and had no energy to quell them this time.

'We've been over this a million times. I'm not up for a bit of fun with you or any other player. I'm here to do a job. I've done what I can and I'm going to copy these right now. And then I'll pack. And then I'll go.'

She didn't even recognise her own voice. A husky crackle. She kept her face turned away from him and began to pick up the photos she wanted.

But he grabbed her wrist and turned her round. 'You

know, you've got a lot of stuff in your head that's really holding you back. You throw out an image of a girl who doesn't give a damn, but the minute you think something threatens you, even if you're way off, you fire back. I just don't get it. You must waste so much energy just battling people. Tara! Look at me. Please.'

He held her wrist up between them like some kind of staff. But still she kept her head twisted away. Just give her a couple of minutes and she would be back under control. Just a little distance and a little quiet. She could still remember the breathing techniques from her self-help books. Just a moment and things would settle.

'Tara.'

He was quieter. His voice was calmer. It was as if he was soothing the angry tiger in her soul. But that made it even more difficult. She couldn't look at him at all. Tried to budge her wrist free.

'Would you please let go of me?' Her voice was still a whisper.

But he didn't. He pulled her close to his chest. He held her head steady. He smoothed her hair and almost rocked her in gentle motions. He murmured. She couldn't make out what he said—but it was soft and sweet. She wanted to give in. She really did. She wanted to recline in the warm waters he was drawing her into. But it was too, too hard. She wasn't used to comfort. Had never been used to comfort. Even before the dark days after her grandmother had died they'd been a family of rockets who shot about, never sat still. Noise, energy and action. Or hiding and fearful.

She breathed out a long, slow breath. Felt moisture on her cheeks and at the corner of her mouth.

Heard movement in the house—heels, doors, a change of air.

She stiffened. He gripped her now. As if he was squeezing strength into her. She could open up, absorb it, or do what she knew and fight it off.

The heels came closer and he would not yield.

'Michael! Tara! There you both are! *Darlings.*'

She pushed him back and he let her. Lifted her chin. Wiped quick fingers under her eyes and squeezed out her best smile. Touched a hand to her hair and tilted her jaw. Big eyes. Ready.

CHAPTER SEVEN

ANGELICA LOOKED AS if she was always walking in on scenes like this. Remarkable. Especially because he'd never offered one up before. She floated through the room, smiling like it was Christmas Day, picking up photos and swooning over this cousin or that aunt. Like she'd popped out to mix a cocktail and come back to the room as if it was littered with confetti instead of emotional carnage.

Yep, she was doing well to gloss over the scene. A natural. He'd never so much as given her cause to worry about him or his private life before. Everything was strictly off-limits. Sure, she'd met some of his past lovers. But he had always maintained a careful distance between his sisters and his personal life. Better that way. He didn't really want them getting to know women who were only passing through anyway—it sent out the wrong signal. Like permanency.

Tara was not coping. She hadn't been coping since the cocktail bar. She was all over the place. Maybe it was spending intense time with just one other person. Maybe it was a come down from the party scene she was so hooked on. Maybe she was struggling with her attraction to him. Hey, he wasn't all ego—it was obvious. Like the permanent erection he was trying to tame.

Still, she wasn't the only one who was reeling after what had just happened. Since when did he talk about his mother…to *anyone*? He had to force himself not to close down conversations when Fernanda wanted to talk about her—to find out what she'd been like. It was so sore. Still.

He watched Tara with Angelica. Her cheeks were scarlet and she couldn't keep her hands off her hair—twirling strands round her fingers and patting it as if it had a life of its own. She never even glanced in his direction, but less than ten minutes earlier she had been running her hands over him like she was trying to catch his cologne.

She gathered up that ridiculous pile of photos and settled onto a couch with Angelica. He had to hand it to his sister: she had a knack of smoothing out some very rough edges. And he knew Tara's edges were rough *and* sore.

She had so much going on in her head. So many issues. She wasn't needy, just prickly. Very, very deep and troubled. And she'd put up such high barriers to climb over. For some guy it would be worth it. She was quality—on so many fronts. Her look—not just the obvious, but her whole look—the lips, the full, thick, lustrous hair that she never had her damn fingers away from, her pure blue eyes and her energy. But most of all, now that he knew her a bit better, she had passion and drive and a very, very soft side that she was totally bent on hiding.

It brought out all sorts of feelings in him that he hadn't even known he had. Yep, no doubt about it: she had pulled a number on the public—even on him, now that he thought about it. She was no more a one-dimensional party girl than he was.

He paced over to another couch and sat with his phone, catching up on emails. Well, sort of catching up on emails. There was a bunch of shows being streamed to him for final edits and he'd need to spend a good few hours absorbed in them. Which worked out well. He could hear Angelica work her magic and Tara begin to respond—as if she *hadn't* been teetering on the edge of an emotional abyss just moments before.

The women homed in on a few pictures and Tara's wrist flew across the pages of her sketchbook. He wondered what the images were like—wanted to see for himself. Then the chat seemed to move to fabrics. Not that he was listening. He was watching the shows from his laptop and making notes.

He'd never really taken in the image of fabulous contrast between them—Angelica all poise and control, Tara all energy and movement. Dark serenity versus blonde vitality. He couldn't take his eyes off her—how natural she was with Angelica. How she lit up the daylight-flooded room. Like a string of fairy lights.

Angelica caught his eye. Got up and left the room. Bestowed one of her serene smiles as she passed him.

He was bent double again over the screen, wondering why the hell one of his best guys had decided that fly on the wall documentaries were a good idea. Still it was clear the public were fascinated with some characters. He looked back over at Tara.

'What about your flight? You still heading home tonight?'

The look that arced across the room to him was telling. Watchful. Wary. But it was a connection, nonetheless. She almost shrugged her shoulders as her vivacity seemed to slip away again

'You should stay—at least one more day. Tara, you look tired.'

The feeling that flew through him as he thought of her getting on a plane he didn't really want to name. It just wouldn't be a good idea for her to travel tonight. She needed to get her full energy back, for sure. And he knew that they needed to revisit the energy between them. They needed to see how far it went. He suspected it would be pretty far. She was the most sensual woman he had ever met, and she still had so much to let loose. He'd love to be the one to help her explore the other side. The connection they could build during sex would be off the charts. He knew it. Didn't need to think about it—just knew it.

'I'm going to stay until the morning. But I have a meeting with the bank in the afternoon. I need to get their approval for another loan extension.'

She looked down at her sketchbook, lifted up a few photos and shuffled them into some sort of order. 'Thank goodness Angelica came back when she did, though. I could have taken the wrong turning entirely on what she liked. She's much less classic than I thought.'

'Really? That surprises me. Maybe you're encouraging her to branch out a bit—walk a bit wilder? To be honest, she's never even been adventurous with her breakfast cereal before. No bad thing as far as I was concerned—you know, as her guardian. Viewing any risk-taking behaviour in my sister was never going to be my favourite hobby.'

'That I can understand.'

'You can?' He found that interesting. She'd accused him of being a control freak where his other sister was concerned. 'What's brought on that change in attitude?'

'Oh, I don't know. Maybe seeing things a bit more from your perspective. I suppose you've got your responsibilities. The only responsibility I have is to myself.'

'That's all most people your age have. You're not unique. It was all *I* had until the accident. If that hadn't happened I still might be in that mind space.'

Which was entirely true. Funny how life could completely switch course within a heartbeat. And, strangely, he was getting that feeling again. He clicked 'pause' on his laptop and walked over to her. Idly lifted and laid some of the photos that now seemed to be in the 'chosen' pile. Glanced at her sketchbook.

'May I?'

She looked a bit tense. In fact she looked crazy tense.

She covered up the sketches with her arms. 'Ah, I'd rather not. I'm a bit…possessive of my work until I'm satisfied with it. It's just a… They're just…'

'They're just parts of you that you'd rather not show the world until you're fully satisfied that you've hidden yourself behind all your walls of hair, make-up, clothes and attitude? You edit your own productions even more than I do, *querida*. Hey, I'm not criticising,' he said, realising that she wasn't exactly looking delighted with his analysis.

He so, *so* wanted to keep her spirits high today. Having seen last night the range of her emotions, he knew that she was so easy to tip into anger and passion. And it was the passion he wanted to see in her again. Those kisses they'd shared before Angelica came home—

sweet and sexy. And she'd been so alive in his arms. Until she'd taken fright again. She was like a little feral cat—defensive, beautiful, hard to catch. But the challenge to tame her was building in him.

He reached out and stroked her hair—the gentlest touch…she could have barely felt it.

'I'm not criticising at all. It's who you are, it's what you are, and only you know the story of you. Which is fine. No one, least of all me, is going to press you for details you don't want to share. But, Tara…' He quietened his voice, watched her soften before his eyes. 'There's something between us. Something—I don't know what. But I don't want to waste any more time battling with you. I want to spend the rest of the time we have here in a whole different place than the war zone we've been in. What do you say? Hmm?'

He tipped up her chin and drank in the blue depths of her eyes. What a face. So honest and open for the briefest of moments. Then she dipped her eyes and hid herself away again.

'I think we've had our chance at that kind of zone, Michael. And I think you know how I feel. You can't lift me and lay me, with *lay* being the operative word.'

She still wasn't looking at him. He let his fingers trail slowly off her jaw. Absorbed the softness, the ridge of her jawbone from the point of her rounded chin to the perfect pink lobe of her ear. She stifled another shudder. He saw it. And it fired him. He was going to be inside her tonight if it was the last thing he did.

'Darlings, are we ready to have some food?'

Sometimes his sister could be a total pain in the butt.

'I've organised some light dishes on the terrace. But I'm afraid I can't join you.'

Or maybe not.

'What's up, Angel? The United Nations been on the phone again? Is there another crisis at a make-up counter?' He deliberately left his hand on Tara's shoulder as he stood behind her. Close. He felt her shift to move away from him—especially, he'd bet, because Angelica was right on it—but he wanted to set her mind at rest.

'Ha-ha, Michael.' Angelica took out her phone and waggled it at him. 'No special envoy missions, but I do have to attend a function with my future husband tonight. Sebastian is feeling sadly neglected. Tara, I hope you don't mind me leaving again so soon, but maybe you have enough to get on with the sketches?'

'That's exactly what I'll do. And I'll see you back in London in maybe two weeks. I'll email you, of course, before then. We can narrow down what you like and then take it from there. I've loved this, Angelica, I really have. It's been so helpful.'

She stood and the girls hugged. Not the usual fashion set kiss-the-air-next-to-the-air nonsense, but proper affectionate hugs. It took him aback. Surely she was just one of Angelica's projects—nothing to get worried about. Nothing to do with the fact that he had been deliberately touching her less than thirty seconds earlier. That had been for Tara's benefit, to keep her on the up. Last thing he wanted was his sister reading anything more into it.

'You want to eat now? Maybe go out later—since it's your last night? Fern is going to be staying at school all week. So there's not a problem if you want to just chill. Work on your sketches? Or I could cook later—another option. Just let me know what suits you, Tara.'

Angelica had gone and the air had settled back down. It was just the two of them again. No staff, no noise. She turned where she stood. Her blue eyes so vibrant in her face. Her cheeks were flushed and her lips were plump and parted.

The urge to grab her was immense and he walked to her. 'You've finished sketching, right?'

She looked down at her piles of paper. 'I think I've done enough for now.'

He could almost feel her wavering. She knew he was bursting to touch her again. But he also knew that they needed some kind of honesty before she would go back there with him. Kissing was one thing. But she was right. He wanted more of her—much more of her. But here. Now. End of.

There was no way this could be repeated because it didn't fit in with his life. And he didn't fit in with her life either. So maybe the best thing would be to have that discussion and then get down to exploring the depths of their chemistry. That way everyone was walking into this with full disclosure and there could be no hurt on her part. And no need to revisit anything on his.

'Tara.'

Just her name. But even that brought a crackle of passion to the air. She looked up sharply. Narrowed her eyes at him. No doubt she was trowelling bricks into place even as she stood there. No time to lose.

'I really want us to finish what we started. I need to. I think you need to, too.'

She touched the chair next to her and he saw her fingers curl round its back. 'I think I need distance from you, Michael, not closure.'

'I know I hurt you. But that's more because of your

imagination than anything I ever did. Sure, I was off hand when I first met you. You're not my type—on paper you're not my type at all. All I did was try to ignore that. But the minute we were alone in the car, and then in my apartment… Tara, I can't keep my hands off you. Look at you—look at what your body does to me. I'm aching, just standing next to you. Just knowing that we have a last few hours together. You do things to me that I can't ignore any more.'

Her eyes were wide and dark. She was ready for him. He looked over to her, caressed her with his eyes—couldn't stop himself if he tried. The tight silk blouse she wore showed him everything that was going on with her body. Her perfect rosy nipples were fully erect and straining through whatever underwear she was wearing. Her chest was heaving with deep, uneven breaths and he knew as he trailed his eyes further down that she was going to be as ready for him as he was for her.

An electric storm seemed to have filled the room.

She'd stopped building her wall.

One more minute and he'd knock the whole thing down.

'You know how it feels when we're together, Tara. Our mouths fit. I've never kissed anyone the way I kiss you.'

She nodded. There was no way she could deny it. Their kisses were dynamite.

'Your skin is like silk, and when I run my hands over any part of you it makes me want to follow it with my mouth. I want to lick and touch and kiss my way over every inch of you, Tara. And that hasn't happened yet. It needs to happen, Tara. Take your blouse off. Let me see that skin. Please.'

She put her fingers to the sides of her blouse and began to finger the long strands of silk that tied it together. His eyes fell to her chest, to the creamy cups that were now being uncovered. He could not imagine anything he wanted to do more than touch her, hold her, and make her cry with pleasure as he fixed his mouth round each of those firm nipples.

He walked a step closer. 'You look so beautiful.'

But she stopped. Stepped back. 'Michael—this is… it's too much. It frightens me. *You* frighten me with what you do to me. What you can make me do even when I know what you really think of me.'

He had it. Finally. The way in.

He shushed her. Shook his head and lifted her jaw into his hands. Gazed down at those bright blue open eyes. 'Tara—what I *really* think of you? I think that you're an amazing girl. *Amazing.* I respect what you've done in your life. Your bright, quick mind and your unending energy. You know I love your body. I can't believe myself how much. But we have to be open. We're on different life tracks. That's all. And, yes, I've been a fool the way I've tried to put that across, but that's all it is. This body of yours screams to me. I've got to have it, Tara. We've got to explore this while we're together. That's not wrong. Not wrong at all. It's all right. All good.'

And he dipped and tasted her mouth. Let his lips find its form and trace its path. Snaked his tongue inside and trailed it to meet hers. Duelled with it. Absorbed the sensations coursing through her, knowing that she was being washed clean with hot sexual energy and that she wasn't fighting back the tide any more. She was with him, moaning into his mouth and grinding her hips into his.

His erection responded, throbbing with pleasure, and he fought the urge to rip their clothes off right there. He ran his hands over her bare flesh, unhooked her bra and filled his palms, watched her head fall back and took his mouth down that pale column, sliding kisses and tongue. Eating her.

'Bedroom—now.'

Dark, sensually drugged eyes closed for a moment when he scooped her up. She was soft and warm in his arms. Precious. He got through doors and up to his bedroom. She held on to him and slid down him. And then she became a wildcat. Her hands were all over him, tearing at his clothes. He helped her—ripped his shirt off, tore everything else off.

She dropped to her knees and took him. Mouth wrapped right round his erection and tugged softly but expertly. He groaned out loud and ran his hands through her hair, pulled her up sharply before it was all over. She looked wanton and wild. Half crazed. Her flesh was pink and damp with perspiration already. She was still half clothed and he needed to see all of her. Both of their hands landed on her waistband and he left her to tug off her trousers while he filled his mouth and hands with every other part of her.

Finally she was ready—naked, half lying back on the bed. Her perfect breasts were bared and the V between her thighs screamed for his mouth. He opened her legs and ran a finger to feel her wetness, knowing it would turn him on even more to see how lost she was in him. And just that touch, that feeling of her, so swollen and wet—it undid him.

Where were the condoms? It felt like life or death—he was so far gone. He fumbled to find them and quickly sheathed himself.

'Tara, I've got to do this. Can't hold on—you're driving me—'

And he found her and plunged in. Felt her heat close around him and squeeze him. He rode her, looking down at her beautiful face, her eyes open, watching him. And that turned him on even more. She was pulling his orgasm out already. He couldn't stop. She was the best. She felt so good, so right. He felt the moment switch—knew there was no going back—and he was shooting inside her as he'd never done before.

He collapsed onto her, still hard, still breathing as if his heart was about to burst. But he knew she needed him and he raised himself up on his elbows. Looked down on her. Felt he was looking right inside her. And what he saw was just *right*. Strangest thing, but that was the only way he could call it. He kissed her long and slow. Poured that feeling right in there. And it was as if he was buoying her up.

She took it, and loved it, and it was she who took charge. She slid out from under him and he rolled over. Then she climbed above him, rested her knees on either side of his head and dipped herself down on him. He was instantly hard again. Had never seen or felt anything more erotic. He pulled her hips just where he wanted them and tasted her, turned her inside out with his tongue. He touched himself and knew that the minute she came he wanted her all over again. She was heaven. And hearing her scream out her orgasm made him feel more of a man than anything he could remember. She was wild. She was beautiful. She was all woman.

He brought her down to him and kissed her exhausted face and chest and stomach and legs, and then he resheathed himself and found the core of her again. They lay together, sliding across one another. Two bodies that somehow seemed to have fused. Two mouths wildly tasting and kissing and two hearts beating the fervour of this passion.

He opened his eyes and knew she had just done the same. Something bigger than sex was happening between them. He would deal with it. He couldn't name it, but he would deal with it. Touching her inside and out right now was all he could do. And he did it until he felt her build to another orgasm, and then he held back, had to feel her clench around him. *Had* to. And the moment came with some sort of primordial power. He burst inside her, throbbing his release over and over again. The wildest, wildest time of his life.

'Tara…' He smoothed her hair and nestled her in his arms. She was molten. And he was going to make sure that she didn't feel anything but cherished right now. They lay panting, flesh cooling. 'That was…'

He laughed. Rolled her under him. Stared at her. She closed her eyes. Laughed back. Empty. He knew then that she was withdrawing. He could feel it.

'You were—you are—so sexy, so beautiful.'

'But still inappropriate.' A hoarse whisper. Hardly heard.

He stilled. 'Tara… Why?' Her face was turned to the side. He grabbed her jaw. 'Why would you sabotage what we've just done?'

She kept her eyes squeezed tight shut and her mouth

formed a tight line. Her body was withdrawing and he saw her rebuilding her defences.

'Tara. You need help. Your mind is so damaged. That was…it was beyond amazing. On so many levels. There was nothing inappropriate about it. It was one hundred per cent special and right.'

She had opened her eyes but they were staring ahead, at nothing. She said nothing.

He was still inside her—he eased off her but held her as close as he could. Didn't matter. She was gone. Away. Curled up against his chest with a thirty-foot wall around her. He stroked her hair, kneaded her arm, murmured how sweet she was.

Nothing. What damage had been done to this girl to make her act like this? Was it his responsibility to find out? He couldn't leave her like this. It was beyond terrible.

But she took the decision away from him. Got up. Spoke into the air.

'Michael, you are a great guy. A great brother to your sisters. And I have had the best of times here. But, really, I think that maybe us doing that was a mistake. As you said, we're on different life tracks. So, thanks. For a good time—a great time. But I'm going to get ready now—if you could get a car sorted? I need to get my plan ready for the bank. I've got those sketches to finish. I have to see what I need to do for Paris. I have so much to organise. Can't believe it—should've made a list.'

He watched, transfixed. She moved around, her beautiful body still naked, picking up clothes, running her hand through her hair. She made it to the door. Opened it, turned to look over one shoulder and drop the most fake smile he could ever remember seeing. Coy, and sexy as Marilyn. And easily as damaged.

Just what had he done? What had he become involved in? And how did he sort it out? She needed someone. His mind was rolling. She needed to talk through what was poisoning her mind. She needed to be looked after—simple as that. She was the most vulnerable creature with the most impenetrable front.

And he was letting her walk right out of his life.

CHAPTER EIGHT

THE BANKERS WERE FREAKS. Worse than she expected. And as for that half-assed so-called business consultant who had drafted the worst business plan... OK, so maybe she should have checked it over herself first. Or used a genuine recommendation rather than a favour from a friend of a friend, when—let's be honest—she didn't really have any of those. Party people were great in the good times. But as soon as your tank ran dry or your credit ran out they vanished faster than champagne at a free bar.

She'd have been better giving the five-hundred-pound fee straight to the Selfridges beauty counter, because she was already planning which totally unnecessary products she was going to have to buy as an upper after this brutal meeting. She closed her eyes and mentally picked her way across the ultra-bright pigmented eyeshadows that she knew already she was going to love—for about two weeks. And maybe some of the winter nail colours...she looked down at her destroyed cuticles, maybe not.

The lecture continued. The terms were being agreed. She should have brought her accountant, but that would have been more money. She could suffer this. She checked her watch. Saw the purple bruise on her arm. A finger-mark. Well, that was what happened when you had wild sex with the hottest man in Europe.

Her heart lurched again.

How many times could she take that sickening feeling that started at her diaphragm and swelled into her chest?

'Are those terms agreeable, Miss Devine?'

'Do I have any choice?'

'Of course. You can walk out of here and see if you can find better terms elsewhere.'

She crossed her legs. Her skirt rode up and she didn't give a damn. Her hold-up stockings were just the thing to make her feel that she had an advantage, because she could predict where their stupid eyes would fall and that gave her some small sense of satisfaction. Even as they looked down their conservative noses at her.

'Yes, I'm sure I could. However, let's not pretend that you've not hiked the rate up because you know my back's against the wall and the clock's ticking.'

She took the paperwork that appeared and signed her name. Stood. Smoothed down her purple silk jersey mini-dress that really didn't need any smoothing. Offered her hand to first one then the other of these sweaty-palmed loan sharks and bolted.

That was one thing ticked off the list. The rest of the list was actually a blur. *Everything* was pretty much a blur. She knew she had some last-minute calls to make, and she wasn't sure about some of next week's details around transportation, and there was a niggle at the back of her head about some deal she'd negotiated with a blogger.

This just wasn't like her. She was usually so on top

of everything. And since she'd got back from Barcelona she'd been on top of nothing. In fact she wasn't even in the middle of things. She felt as if she'd run headfirst into a wall and was now lying at the bottom in a pile of rubble. She was physically exhausted, mentally exhausted, and—hold the front page—emotionally exhausted. It didn't even feel like a come down. It felt as if the universe had reordered itself and she was spinning off alone into some other cosmos with no control and no way back.

She tripped down Oxford Street, eyes up, seeing nothing. Heading to offload some cash. Finding solace in crowds. *Again*. When had that started? Heading home from school via every shop or friend's house so that the journey never ended? Staying out of the way when she knew Grandpa Devine would be home before her? Leaving by the back door when he came in the front? Plotting and planning her escape. Dreaming of when *she* would be the one in control, not him. When she didn't need to rely on anyone other than herself for anything.

And she had achieved that. As soon as she'd hit London she'd known that the world was hers now. Maybe one day she would loosen up and share some of the control with someone else, but she was still far too raw for that yet.

So what had she been thinking, getting into bed with Michael Cruz again? Of all the stupid, *stupid* things to do. It wasn't as if he hadn't taken up nearly all of her headspace just by being in the same house as her, and now for her to have placed her holiest of holies back in his possession… She had no one else to blame for this monumental downer.

She shoved open doors and involuntarily offered her wrist to the first perfume girl. She hated flowery perfumes. It was a flowery perfume. She sniffed it. *Yuk.*

Her phone lit up in her bag. Her eyes widened in hope—but, no. It was a message from a publicist friend who sometimes worked with her. There was a party tonight with a lot of key players. There was a hot young Danish boy with plenty of family cash in town, looking to bankroll some 'assets'. Tara should get herself to Shoreditch and see if she couldn't persuade Lars that investing in Devine Designs would provide all the assets he would ever need.

Tara's heart sank. She should be pleased. This was a genuine opportunity. But the thought of it just exhausted her. All over again. What to wear, how to travel, how long to stay, how much to drink, who to chat to—the list went on. And all she wanted to do was soak in a bath and curl up in bed. But even that was a lie. She wanted nothing more on this earth than to lie in the arms of Michael Cruz.

The sex had blown her mind. She knew she'd acted as if it was even more pastel than vanilla. In fact, she'd told him that it was worse than 'passable'. Had she really said that? To the man who had taken so much time over her? Who had relentlessly shown her care and concern, even trusted her with his secrets? Was she that much of a terrible person herself that she had to deliberately hurt him to keep him away from her? And that had worked *so* well!

She walked on through the throng. She was even more of hypocrite than he was. She should be ashamed of herself for her lack of integrity.

Her phone flashed again. She sat on a make-up bar

high chair to read the message. Her heart flew, hoping it was from Michael. Her heart sank when she saw it wasn't. Feared the worst and so it came. There were more capital problems. The transportation costs had been raised. She hadn't nailed that side of the deal and it was coming back to bite her.

There was no more scope at the shark bank. So the party. She sighed from her soul. *Here we go again.*

By the time the fourth glass of actually pretty good-quality fizz had hit the back of her throat Tara had decided that she had nothing left to lose. She was back in her scene. She could mope about. She could play hunt the celebrity—the *real* celebrities. She could flirt with Lars—except she couldn't find him. Or she could just drown her sorrows. Like a sackful of unwanted kittens. Boy, she was feeling sorry for herself!

She checked her phone. A complete waste of time. She had been more than clear with Señor Cruz that he was the last person she wanted to hear from. So why did her sad little heart sink every time she performed this sad little ritual? He was not going to contact her because she'd done everything in her power to push him away. She hated that she could cut people off at the knees. Hated to hurt anyone. *Ever.* But it was who she'd become in this game of hide and seek that she'd started

Another glass. Another scout around the place. A trail to the ladies'. There were so many people offering her things tonight…but nothing that was going to do her any good. The new turquoise eyeshadow was stuck in the creases of her eyes. And it made the whites of her eyes look pink. Or was that the drink? She'd get another. Find Lars. He had to be here.

Stupid shoes. They were too high. She lost her balance and her foot slipped over. Drink spilled on her hand. She licked it.

The glass was taken from her hand. 'Hey!'

'What do you think you're doing?'

It was him. Michael. It was Michael. Her eyes focussed. A little bit. He was so handsome. He was so beautiful. His golden skin over those perfect bones. That smudge of stubble. She put out her fingers to touch his face. He grabbed her wrist.

'Tara. Are you OK? Had enough to drink?'

She just wanted to touch him. 'Hey baby… yes, I'm having a good time! What are you doing here? Have you come to party? You need a drink. Give me mine back and let's go to the bar.'

'I don't think so.'

'Wha…a.. at? Come *on*! There's such lovely fizz, and I spilled mine.'

She reached for her glass but he was being weird and wasn't letting her get it.

'What's wrong?' She pouted.

'Tara—you've had too much to drink.'

She tried so hard to stand straight, but one foot wouldn't find the floor properly. 'I've hardly touched it. Only had two or three…maybe four. Five. Oh, come on, Michael, its a party and I have to find Lars. Give me my drink.' She swung out an arm to get her glass but he was still being such a killjoy.

'Who the hell is Lars?'

Who the hell *was* Lars? 'I don't know. Some guy. With money. For me.'

'What? He owes you money?'

That was funny. She laughed—a bit too hard—and fell against Michael again. It was so nice to fall against him.

She held onto his shirt. 'Cruz…'

But he took her by the arms and held her away from him. 'Tara. Sober up. Tell me again—what's the deal with this guy? Does he owe you money?'

'No.' She did sober up then—for a moment. 'I'm broke. My business is broke. I went to the bank and they gave me some money but not enough. But Lars… wherever he is…he wants some "assets"—ha-ha. And I have assets, Michael. Don't I?'

Oh, that had been the wrong thing to say. Even though it was hard to focus on him completely, she could see and feel that he didn't like that.

'Your assets are not up for debate. And you're not going to stay here drinking—with Lars or anyone else.'

'But it's early. It's…' She tried to focus on her watch. It looked like it was only one a.m. Far too early to go home. Some people wouldn't even have arrived yet. 'It's early, Michael. And I need to stay for just a li'l longer. There might be some good publicity too. And I really need it now.'

'You don't need to get publicity this way, Tara. There are other ways to promote yourself and your business.'

'Yeah, but…' she poked at his chest with her new nails '…this way is free. And it suits who I am. '

What a look he was giving her. Like she was a real disappointment. 'We can talk about that. Let's go.'

His touch was crazy strong. He scooped her close and put his arm round her. That felt good. But then he marched her, and her feet just wouldn't do what she wanted them to do.

'Michael. Slow, baby. I can't keep up.'

She almost went over on her ankle, so he scooped her in harder, until she was plastered right down his side and she didn't need to use her feet at all.

'Wheeeee!' She giggled as she was scooted along. 'You're so strong…' But then they went to the stairs and not the bar, and she realised that he was heading out… 'Michael. Where…? What…? Hey, I can't go. I told you—I need to find Lars!'

'Yeah? Well, we can talk about that too.'

'Michael, put me down.'

This wasn't funny any more. Cold air hit her bare arms and thighs. He still held her clamped to his side. There were paps about and their flashes and catcalls sounded. She started to struggle against him. That feeling of being powerless was taking over. Didn't feel good. *At all.*

A car door opened and he put her inside, then jammed himself in beside her. 'Drive.'

The car moved off. Fast. She jolted to the side. She was really beginning to sharpen up now.

She turned to him, her voice choked with fury, furred with alcohol. 'What the hell is all this about? Just who do you think you are, dragging me about like you own me?'

He stared straight ahead, his jaw clamped and his mouth worked into a tight line. No way was he going to sit there in silence. Not after that disgusting display of machismo.

'I mean it, Michael. What do you think you're doing? Didn't you see the snappers? They were all over the place. I'm going to look like an idiot tomorrow.'

Swift turn of head then. 'You'd have looked like a bigger idiot if you'd stayed on in that club. You're drunk.

You're alone. And you were cruising the place for men with money. What on earth are you playing at, Tara? You're asking for trouble—and who knows how you've managed to escape so far? So you can consider this a favour. No need to repay.'

'I decide what I do and what favours I call. Not you! You're nothing to do with me! What's wrong? Have you run out of sisters to bully?'

He shook his head at her and stared straight ahead again. But there it was again. He actually thought she was just another little girl to order about. He hadn't so much as stopped to ask her if she even wanted his help. Maybe she should lighten up and let him? After all, he could solve her problems in a heartbeat. But really? Had she put all that effort in over all the years just so that she could pimp herself out down his version of Easy Street?

'You can look down your nose at me all you want, but I've managed to survive perfectly well up until now by doing things my way. So you can tell your driver to turn the car around. I've got business to attend to.'

'Business? Dressed like that? Full of drink? Not a chance.'

She was sobering up at lightning speed now. She leaned forward. 'Driver. Can you let me out, please?'

She saw the driver's eyes flick to Michael's in the mirror. The car didn't even slow down.

'You're coming to my apartment. You can have a business meeting there. When you've sobered up.'

'You know, you've got serious control problems. Do you really, *really* think that I'm going to just walk out of this car and up to your apartment? Because you *tell me to*? And dressed like *what*, exactly? What's that supposed to mean?'

He sat there. Didn't move. Didn't even seem to have heard her. It was as if she was insignificant. Irrelevant.

'Are you even *listening* to me?'

He turned his head. Just a bit. Looked at her out of the corner of his superior eyes. As if that was all she merited.

'I'm listening to a woman who isn't capable of rational thought because she's too drunk. So let's keep the sartorial chat until the morning.'

'The morning? *The morning?* You actually think I'm going to spend the night with you?'

'No, I don't, Tara. Not in the way *you* think. I wouldn't take advantage of any woman who was as out of control as you are. It's not my style.'

'Yeah? Well, I wouldn't let you near me tonight if my life depended on it.' She tried to hiss at him, but it came out in a jumble and made her feel even more furious—with herself and with him. 'Oh, you know what I'm trying to say.'

'Just about. But that's fine—it's sorted, then. You can sleep in the guest room and then in the morning we can talk about your business.'

Still he stared straight ahead, as if looking at her was going to make him lose his lunch—or whatever meal he'd last eaten. He was so arrogant. Really, it was all she could do not to slap him. *Hard*.

She looked down at her dress. There was nothing wrong with it. Well, nothing that a ton of accessories better than she could afford could fix. To be honest… it was way past its season. And its sell-by date. In fact a firelighter and a pyromaniac could sort the whole lot out in a heartbeat. She really was looking awful. And that eyeshadow. What had she been thinking?

The car braked and lurched. A crowd of drunken girls had spilled off the pavement onto the road, squealing and laughing. They looked as drunk as her. She was knocked into the door as the driver swerved to avoid them. Michael slid against her and she yelped. He was right there. Warm breath on her cheek.

'Tara! Are you OK?'

His whole weight had smashed against her as the car turned and she felt him jerk back, fold his arms around her, scoop her close to his side, comfort her. There it was again. That feeling of letting herself sink into him. Into the warm tropical waters of his presence. So easy. Would be so easy to let go. But she mustn't. Must never give in. Must keep him back. Never let him get her heart. Or her mind. He'd had her body. Her body loved his body. But he would never have her mind. *Never.*

'Tara…'

He was smoothing her hair, her cheek. Kissing her cheek. Holding her head as if it was a glass egg. She shoved at him.

'Fine. I'm fine.'

The car stopped. She wasn't fine. She was shot. Shattered. Too much stress, too much drink and too much emotion had decked her like sucker punches. The end of the road. Felt like she wanted to sleep in a layby. Just until this next lot of emotional traffic passed by. So tired. So, so tired. She rested her head in her hands, her elbows on her knees.

The door opened. He was there. Arms, body, warmth, strength. She was lifted. Held. Secure.

Her head fell against his chest. Every part of her felt contained. She loosened and let go. Treacle in his arms.

He carried her through the space to his apartment.

She felt the changes in the air, felt his heartbeat against her cheek, felt the solid wall of his chest and the solid wall of *him*. Man. Just pure man. And for the first time in her life she accepted it.

'How do you do this to me?' she whispered into him. Didn't know if he could hear her, but it didn't matter. 'How do you make me melt when I want to stay so strong? I need to *not* melt. I don't want to be soft—and sad. I don't want to be like her, Michael. I wish you could see that.'

He opened the door to a room that was silver. And white. Brittle light from a sparkling chandelier. A large white bed stuffed high with pillows. Gently laid her down. Sank into the softest mattress. Felt it envelop her. Felt a soft, heavy quilt wrap around her. Felt the cloak of sleep steal over her. Darkness.

CHAPTER NINE

TARA AWOKE TO more darkness. A tight, tight band of pain across her head. Pressure from where she had lain all night in the same position. The quilt had fallen away but she was warm. She turned on to her back, pulled the quilt over her and just lay there. What had happened?

A knock on the door and then it swung open. Michael walked in. She squinted at him through the hand that was nursing her head. He looked amazing. Jeans and a shirt. Tall and impossibly handsome. He glanced at her and then made it to the window. With a whoosh the blind went up and daylight seared her vision.

'Wow, the sun's up, then?' Her voice was hoarse and crackly.

'For a good few hours, yes.' He walked to the bed. Placed a glass of water on the table beside her.

She shuffled and leaned up on her elbows, but the pain in her head was immense. Had to flop back down again.

'Feeling less than perfect?'

She kept her hand over her eyes. 'Slightly. Can't you shut the blind again? That's just cruel.'

He sat down on the bed. She felt his weight and sank towards him a bit. 'You've got a strange view of cruelty, Tara. Imagine how you'd be feeling if you'd stayed there even longer.'

'Yeah, but I didn't.' She hadn't wanted to go at all, but she'd forced herself. For… *Lars!* 'Dammit!' She sat straight up in bed and winced at the axe through her eyes. 'What time is it anyway?' Maybe there was an after-party somewhere. 'Where's my phone?'

It was worth a text—she had such little time left to get anything sorted before she had to start shipping clothes to Paris.

He handed her the bag which was sitting at her feet. She scrabbled through it—pulled out her phone. Dead. 'Ah, no! I've got no power!' She looked up at Michael. 'Have you got a charger for this?'

'Tara. Calm down and drink your water.'

'But I could be missing something. That guy—Lars. I never got a chance to meet him. Haven't you got a charger for this? I thought you had the same phone as me?'

He shook his head. Stood up.

'Where are you going?'

He didn't turn round—just walked to the door. 'To get a different perspective on life.'

She looked at his disappearing back. 'What the hell is that supposed to mean?' No response.

What did he mean? What other perspective was there when your business was going down the tubes? Closely followed by your life. If she didn't get this sorted she risked everything she'd gained at London Fashion Week. If she didn't have the cash for Paris she wouldn't have the cash to keep going. Period. And that was way bigger than just expanding her business. That was public humiliation. Bankruptcy.

And where did you go when you had no money? Home? With your tail between your legs and your ears full of *I told you sos*? Never! Never, never. Never.

It was all right for him—he had piles of money and piles of contacts. She had…she had… She had the hangover from hell and in one way he was right—it could have been much worse. She reached for the water and took a long, gulping drink. Finished it. And she had dehydration.

This was not going to plan. She had two days left to get more cash. If she got on it now she could maybe, *maybe* see if she could get a meeting set up. Surely there had to be someone interested in funding her? Maybe she'd made some impact last night? She should get online, see what was being reported about the party. There was still time to cash in.

She got out of the nest of a bed, noticed that the putrid eyeshadow had transferred itself to the snow-white linen. Then she caught her own reflection in the large freestanding mirror. Oh, man, she looked like a bouquet of dead flowers! Her hair was sticking up, her face was smeared with make-up and her dress—all forty shades of vibrant neon jungle print—was wrapped around bits of her. Just bits. With the rest of her poking out at various angles—none of them flattering.

She needed a shower. Maybe Michael would have some of his sisters' clothes she could borrow until she got home? Ha-ha—get real. She might just about be able to squeeze into Fernanda's duvet cover.

She went through to the kitchen. It was like a photo shoot for Sunday mornings. High windows, lazy light. Gorgeous guy on a bar stool, papers spread in front of him, espresso cup and half-eaten pastry at his right-hand side. Place set for her. All you could want.

His laptop was open. He glanced up at her, then back to his paper. But his probing eyes saw everything in the two-second body-scan. She hugged herself. She didn't belong in this photo shoot.

'OK if I have a shower?'

'Of course. Though you may want to see these first.' He touched the laptop towards her, then picked up the corner of his paper and his coffee cup, got on with the business of breakfast.

She looked at the screen. 'What is it?'

At first she couldn't make out what she was seeing, but then it registered. It was herself and various others. A photo-montage of the party, with editorial. There were clips of her arriving in Shoreditch. She brightened. She actually looked OK! The dress was not as bad as it had ended up…having been slept in. Hair was fine. Make-up—not so good, but she'd pulled it off—just.

Ew. A back view—her generous bottom, swaying as she walked into the club. 'Oh, well no need to ask if my bum looks big in this.'

Shoes were fine, but definitely too high for a night on the fizz. Then the clips changed. Others entering and leaving. Michael. He walked in looking—the only word for it was *immense*. Dark suit, white shirt, no tie. Face relaxed but eyes intense. A nod to the cameras and right on inside. Suave. It made her want to plant one on him—he was so edible. Just like now. How could one man hold such a full deck of cards? He had absolutely everything going on. Including being the best lover she had ever had. *Ever.*

A glass of juice was placed in her hand. A stool was

nudged towards her. She hoisted herself up onto it, still watching. He went back to his reading. More video of more people. Her publicist friend. Dutch Ronnie. He damn well didn't *look* broke, that was for sure! Then the real A-list arrived. She hadn't seen any of them. Honestly—how hard was it to get an autograph these days?

'Oh, well. Looks like a good crowd. Glad you went?' She knocked the glass against her wonky teeth, dribbled a little juice and wiped her mouth with her hand.

He glanced up at her, then to the screen. 'Keep watching,' he said.

A head shot of a reporter in front of the entrance. Then the camera zoomed to something over his shoulder. And there it was. At first she thought it was a bouncer, throwing someone out, and then she realised it was Michael, dragging *her* out. She looked ridiculous. Tucked under his arm, her legs almost lifeless, shoes trailing on the ground. But it was her face. To describe it as angry would be a kindness, but it was twisted in an ugly scowl. He looked implacable. Even when he put her in the car like a box of old junk.

'Well, you got your wish.' He took another sip of coffee and read another inch of paper.

'*Sorry*?' She was stunned. The reporter laughed into the camera. Behind her the paps were running after the car, training their lenses on it. 'You think I wanted *that* kind of publicity?'

He tilted his face to her in that annoying way he had. 'You *didn't* want that kind of publicity? You want *any* kind of publicity. You've proved that again and again.'

'You honestly think I want to be shown to the world tucked under your arm like a drunk getting ejected by a bouncer?'

'What I honestly think is that last night you didn't seem to care who or what noticed you, as long as someone did—and preferably someone with money. So, lucky for you that I was there. Not only did I notice you, I also have money. And once you have showered and eaten—if your stomach can cope with that—I'm going to sit you down and show you some options for funding. Options that don't include dressing up, drinking and falling about. OK?'

'No! Not OK!' His tone had imperceptibly risen with every word but she pitched in with an extra fifty per cent volume. Just to emphasise her point. 'What makes you think that I want to hear anything you've got to say?'

He nailed her with a full-on stare. She heard her own words echo between them. She was an idiot. She knew she was an idiot. But they were out of her mouth and suspended in the air like day-glo graffiti. He was trying to help her. She could see that. But did he have to be so dominant? So overbearing? So…so much of a man?'

'You know, Tara, for an astute businesswoman you can be pretty damn stupid. But fine.' He gestured with his hands in a motion of defeat. 'Fine. Do what you want. Or don't. It doesn't matter to me. If you want to take the independent female high ground, that's your shout.'

He picked up his paper again.

'You know where the bathrooms are. Help yourself.'

He picked up his phone, pressed in the code and read a message. Put it back down. Gently. Took a bite of his pastry. Ignored her. Completely and utterly.

She sat there. Two words stuck in her throat like dry toast. She couldn't say them. She looked at the screen again. His screensaver had come on but the image of her being put in a car was imprinted in her mind—very, very clearly.

'Surely you can see how that made me look? To be carried from a club and put in a car? Like you were my dad picking me up from a church disco, or something?'

'I don't know, Tara. Because you don't tell me anything. Do you even *have* a dad? Where were you born? I don't know anything about you other than what you choose for the world to know—that you like to drink, and dance, and flirt. That you're a ball-breaker and a risk-taker.'

'Well, I don't know anything about you either! Oh, sure, I know where you were born, and that you went off the rails, then back on them when you…when you became your sisters' guardian. But what have you really told me? Or shown me? What do *you* let anyone know about you? I could have read all that on the internet.'

That got a double-take. The cup that was halfway to his mouth paused. 'Good try, Tara.'

'What do you mean? I'm telling the truth. You're even more of a closed book than I am.'

He finished his coffee. Walked over to the machine and poured some more. Leaned back on the counter and perused her like she was a museum exhibit. 'I mean, good try because you are an absolute master of subterfuge. But I can see right through you. Distract. Divert. Decoy tactics. That's your speciality.'

She frowned. Truly didn't know what he was getting at. 'I'm only being honest.'

He smiled. 'You don't strike me as anything other than honest. I've worked that part out for myself. But you give nothing away. And when the conversation gets anywhere near the real Tara you switch—go on the attack, change the subject.'

'No, I don't! No… I don't…' Her voice trailed off. He didn't need to come back at her. She suddenly heard herself. Wow. She sounded ridiculous. Absolutely ridiculous.

His smile broadened. He pushed himself off from the counter. Put his coffee cup down and walked over to her. Eyes fixed on her the whole time. 'No, of course you don't! You're more defensive than an armed guard.' He braced his arms on either side of the counter where she sat.

She flashed him a grudging half-smile. 'Can't help it.'

'Maybe you should try.'

He put his arms right round her and hugged her into him. She stiffened. For a moment she stiffened. But he wouldn't let go. And then he began his master stroke—his touch. He drew slow circles on her back. Held her and touched her. And eased the tension right out of her. It was heavenly. She should give in. Her body already had.

He lifted her to her feet, cupped her face. Smiled right into her eyes. 'Do you trust me?'

She nodded.

'Enough to let me into your head?'

He held her so steady, stared straight into her eyes. That feeling swelled to her chest again and she knew right then she would refuse him nothing. 'I'll try.'

'Good. I know you'll try. I don't know what's stuck inside you, or what's caused you to be this way, but opening up will help you through.'

He stroked her hair and she found words coming into her throat.

'What do you want to know? That I left home when I was sixteen? Left town. Left the country to come here. Got a place in college and never looked back.'

He smoothed her and soothed her and more words came.

'I had to get away. My life was not good. Not good at all.'

She tucked her head against him, spoke into his chest. She could feel his strength and patience. He wasn't pressuring her, but it was so much for her to pull up these dark buried memories.

'And no, I don't have a dad—not one I ever knew, anyway. I have a granddad. And a mother who "let herself down" and was never allowed to forget it. And neither was I.'

She couldn't say any more. It was like a rock had been shifted. A tiny chink of light was behind it, but the rock was huge and heavy and she had no more energy to push it. She laid her head against him and felt the wetness from her breath on his shirt. His hands had never stopped stroking her. There were no other sounds. Nothing.

'*Soft and sad.* You said that last night. Is that who you were talking about? Your mother?'

She nodded into him, willing him not to ask any more. She couldn't give up any more to him just now. The soothing touch of his hands was like some kind of balm and she absorbed it easily, thankfully.

'OK, baby. OK.'

Long moments passed and then he eased her off him.

Cupped her jaw, smiled. His eyes were kind. Warm, dark and kind.

'You look like a paint palette.'

She smiled back, found her voice again. 'I can only imagine.'

'Want to shower? Together?'

Just those words sent a quiver of passion right through her. She lifted her face to him, desperate for his mouth. 'Now who's offering up distractions?'

'Oh, I think we could distract each other for quite a few hours this morning.'

He placed a kiss on her cheek. Slipped his hand round to her ribs. Slowly raised it to cup the underside of her breast. Palmed it. Touched her nipple. Her sex thrummed to life. He kissed her other cheek. Circled her nipple over and over. She found his mouth. His perfect mouth. It was a full-blown assault. Defence was futile.

He took her hand and she followed him out through the door. They walked down the long, daylight-flooded hallway to his bathroom.

She caught sight of herself in a console table mirror. 'I look horrific. Like a bomb went off in a flower shop.'

'I'm not going to lie to you, Tara…'

She mock-punched his arm. Tried but failed to run her fingers through her hair. 'And *you* look like your usual fragrance advert. So there's no point in competing.'

'Tara Devine? Not competing? Does your publicist know?'

She smiled and laughed. *Ugh*. That had brought her right back down to earth.

She stalled. 'I really need to get back on to this. I need to find another backer, or at least some short-term cash. Otherwise I'm finished. And just as it's all taking off.'

Michael stopped. Spun her round to face him. Held her face again. 'The offer's there, Tara.' He bent forward, kissed her. Slow. Deep. Long. 'And I don't make it lightly.' Kissed her again.

Her mind was beginning to go fuzzy. She couldn't drag her mouth away. Could not get enough of his tongue. Her hands went to his shirt. His hands went to her dress. He ripped it up and over her head. She clawed at his buttons.

'We need to do this. I need to be inside you before I can make another coherent sentence.'

He was out of his shirt now. Bare-chested. The most fabulous defined bare chest she could ever remember seeing. Golden skin and light dusting of dark hair. Pecs that looked too perfect to be real. Musculature that was not too heavy but radiated strength. She dragged her fingers across him, relishing the sensations.

He stilled her wrists and held her arms open, exposing her in her underwear. But she felt his adoration—wave after wave of it—as he looked her over. Then he dipped his head and tugged at her nipple through the silk of her bra, soaking her.

Even though she felt like yesterday's rubbish, she could no more stop this than stop breathing. She held his head in place while he worshipped her breasts. Her legs went weak. Knees buckled. All her blood rushed south.

He stopped and held her close. 'C'mon, let's get dirty.'

Michael watched her towel her hair. Wrapped in a bathrobe that drowned her, and with one leg crossed over the other, she looked strangely at home. And he wanted her all over again.

He had to move away. Had to get some space. He'd lost count of the different ways they'd made love. She brought out sides of him he hadn't known he had. When he got his hands on her—every time since the first time—he just wanted to possess her. It was almost primal. Then he wanted to play with her. Like his very own private movie. And then he wanted to cherish her.

He walked into the kitchen. At least this time she hadn't bolted the minute they'd finished. This time he'd held her in a grip like a vice, completely wrapped his legs and arms around her, tucked her head under his chin and held on. Even then he'd sensed her struggle with the aftermath. And even now he knew that he had only kept her with him physically. Her mind had drifted away.

He wondered how much her head was wholly with him when they made love? There was always that feeling of distance with her.

He was beginning to feel like Angelica. Like Tara was some sort of project. He could rationalise his offer to help her with her business—anyone would do that, especially if there was a quid pro quo, which there would be. And he was about to outline it to her as soon as she had finished fixing her hair. But why was he so caught up in what was going on in her head? What did he care if she gave him the best sex he'd had in years—OK…ever—and then wanted to retreat back to her shell? Wasn't that every single guy's dream?

He flicked on his laptop again. Found the page he was looking for. Looked at the footage. She looked so vulnerable. Even entering the club, she looked not just alone, but lonely. That fabulous smile with the quirky teeth. He could read every one of those smiles now. And the emotions that shone through that one were watchful, guarded and, yes, defensive. She didn't just have her armed guard—she had a whole battalion behind a fortress.

But there was no doubt she was getting closer to letting him in. Whatever hurt she held from growing up in a family where she was seen as something shameful—if that was what she was getting at—it had scarred her pretty harshly. Of course it had. And of course she would haul that about with her and let it shade her life.

That was a lot for anyone to handle. And, to be honest, the fact that she had chosen him to share it with… that was a responsibility he wasn't even sure he should be handling. She needed—she *deserved* somebody who could help her work things through. Maybe even a professional. Because the thing he'd thought he wanted to know—that she wasn't going to rip the heart out of his family, that she wasn't going to turn Fern's head the way his had been turned at that age—was the thing he still wasn't sure about.

He heard her moving about in his house. It didn't feel wrong.

'Morning again, beautiful.'

She walked into the kitchen looking fresh as spring flowers. Her skin was scrubbed clean and flushed pink. Her eyes, even shaded by lilac hangover shadows, were bright. Her halo of crazy peachy blonde hair was tamed. And her smile—her Tara smile—was as natural as he'd ever seen it.

'Morning again, handsome.'

He couldn't help it; he trailed a finger down her

cheek and cupped her face up to him. Dragged a kiss from that sensual mouth and felt intoxicated all over again.

Drugged.

Obsessed.

Not things he wanted himself to be feeling. He really had to get back on track and stop overthinking her and her issues. She spoke to him sexually. OK, she *screamed* at him sexually. That he could handle. But all this analysis and worry that she was beginning to generate in him…?

He had enough to be getting on with—with the increasingly smart-mouthed Fernanda. He had to remember what his main responsibility was. Yes, he would help Tara, but he really had to get a grip and not lead her into thinking that this was anything more than what it was. Confessions about her mother might be the very thing to help her move on—but they came with flashing blue lights. He had to pause this and work with his own family before he could help anyone else work out theirs.

He was not himself. This was not how he handled his life. Dammit but he had to get a grip.

'You got your business suit on under that robe?'

She beamed up at him. 'Of course. Do you want to check?'

'Ah… I think we'd better leave your outerwear in place for the duration of this meeting.'

He turned his laptop round to her, found the site he was looking for. 'There you are. Have a look at this and then we'll talk.'

She squinted at the screen. Then up at him. 'What is it?'

'It's how you can promote yourself, earn yourself

a truckload of money, and not have to sell so much of yourself in the process.'

He knew he wasn't missing and hitting the wall, but she had to know that her ways were not the wisest.

'It's a new line one of my production companies is moving with. Taking "behind the scenes" web productions forward and doing a more in-depth take on some subjects. Fly on the wall, if you want to use that expression. Very special subjects. And, in your particular field, the links you could develop with other associated businesses could be very, very lucrative. Way beyond product placement.'

She sat still. Super-still.

'What do you think?'

Not a sound. He waited. Filled nobody's silence in business. Ever.

He got up and moved to get some coffee. The silence swelled, broken only by domestic noises—coffee sploshing, fridge door creaking, a swallow sounded loud in his head.

Finally...slowly... 'I think... I'm not sure...but I think I love it.'

He swallowed more coffee, watched her as she scrolled through the site.

'It could be perfect. How long would the cameras be there?'

'That all needs to be discussed. And, remember—it's not me you'd be dealing with.'

She looked up at him. 'Oh? Who, then?'

'This is new for us. And, to be honest, it wasn't my favourite idea. But I think it could work well for you. It's been brought across from a company we've acquired. The producer's an easy guy to work with.'

'I think it could be the perfect vehicle, but I'd need to be really sure how it would all roll. I mean…' She looked up at him, excitement writ large on her face. Her eyes sparkled. 'It's a good offer. A *great* offer. I suppose my only worry would be how much control would I have? You know…you hear of these things. People get sucked in. Start to show themselves. And then the final edit is out of their control. They end up being made to look like a fool, or they totally open up and their whole persona is gone.'

'The persona that you've created that is actually nothing like you? Are you afraid people might see a woman with drive and talent—a real human being? Worried that they might see the real you, Tara? Whoever that is.'

'That's not fair. You're just as much of a two-face as me.'

He absorbed that one. Let it sink in. She had a point in some ways, but so much of his life was an open book. Facts—and fiction—were available, as she'd said, on every internet search engine. He couldn't have lived the life he'd led and expected otherwise. But nobody really knew what had gone on in his head. No one had any notion how bad the carnage had been. Not even Angelica. And certainly not Fern.

'You've tried that before, Tara. This isn't about me. But I don't have anything to hide. I'll tell you whatever you want to know. Ask away.'

For a moment she looked as if she was about to. She looked up from the screen and right into his eyes. Her mouth formed a question but the words didn't come. He cocked his head in a question of his own, but she closed her lips and went back to the screen.

'I think this would be a good chance to let the spotlight shine for just a moment on something other than the hedonism, Tara. Editorial control? I'm not going to promise you would have control, but I will promise that you will not be made out to be anything other than what you are.'

He could feel her internal squirm starting up. It would be a major step forward for her if she could.

'You know that I use the media. That's no secret. But I'm not a big enough name for them to follow me everywhere, so when I do pop up it's exactly how I want it to seem, I suppose...'

'This isn't sensationalist, if that's what you're worried about. It's art. I'm not in the business of offering free advertising. So what you need to ask yourself is if you're comfortable with who you are in the downtime, when your beautiful smile and party antics aren't there to keep everyone at bay. I'm not talking about showing yourself warts and all, I'm just suggesting adding another dimension. And, Tara, if you can, if you're able to show people more of how you get your muse, how you organise your business, then people will warm to you and your profile will rise. All good.'

She nodded. He could see every thought fly over her face as she worked it through.

'It still doesn't solve my cash-flow problems. My immediate need, five-grand-right-now, cash-flow problems.'

'Not in itself. But I'm sure a contract with us would go a major way towards releasing funds. Hell, I don't mind taking a look at your business plan, seeing if I can't make it a bit more appealing.'

He felt so responsible for her on one level—she was

his sisters' friend, a family friend. And she was his lover. For now. For today. Who knew where that would end up? But most of all she was a single girl in a big world with a lot of talent who just needed a little direction. Anyone in his position would help out.

He could give her the cash right now—but if he even suggested that he knew what would happen next. And he definitely wasn't going to force the issue. If she didn't want to bite, he wasn't going to lose sleep over it.

'Ah. I don't know. I really don't.' She sat running her fingers through her hair, twisting it over and over. 'It could be good—it could be great! But you've already said that I wouldn't have editorial control. I mean, what if I come across as a neurotic freak? What if it turns into one of those "how many bugs can the crazy girl eat" shows? I've been marketing myself in a whole different direction. That's not who I am.'

'But that's the whole point, Tara—do you *know* who you are? Does anybody?'

She looked startled for a moment, but then the defensiveness returned. 'Good question, Michael. Do you?'

'I'll tell you right now who I am—I'm a survivor. And a damned lucky one at that. I was born to two parents who loved each other, and but for the world my father was caught up in they might still be together. But they're not.' He paused. Hearing himself speak about this out loud was almost shocking. She was the only woman he had ever spoken to about his parents before. And for some reason he trusted her enough to take the lead.

'I'll tell you it all, Tara—open book. Is that what you want to hear? Will that help you?'

She was wide-eyed, watching him.

'For years my mother and I were a team. Then when she met Carlos I felt abandoned. All over again.'

She reached out an arm to him.

'It's fine. I had hours of therapy—enforced therapy—to help me see that. I was sent to therapy even before I needed it, that's how considerate a mother she was.' He laughed—an almost bitter-sounding laugh. But he wasn't bitter. He was lucky. 'Then I landed big jobs on the teen acting and modelling circuit. The shallow, vacuous world of how good everyone looks and how fake everyone is.'

'Is that why you're so against Fernanda getting involved?'

He knew he was getting near to dangerous territory, but she deserved to know. It wasn't personal, anything against Tara—it was loathing and fear of how that world could corrupt. Because *he* had first-hand knowledge.

'Yes. But more than the pointlessness of that 'industry', for want of a better word, it's the side issues—the drugs, the drink, the parties.'

'And you think that I represent all of that? You think that I'll corrupt Fernanda and lead her into a life of debauchery?'

He shrugged. 'I did. But I was seeing what you wanted me to see—what you want the world to see.' He moved towards her—her and her scrubbed-clean naturalness that no one ever saw. 'You're not that person, Tara, but you're still in that world. And you might be able to stay in control and manipulate the world to suit you, but others can't. I couldn't.'

'Yes, but you were—what?—sixteen?'

'Exactly.'

'And you made your own choices. I made my own choices at sixteen. You're not giving her a chance.'

'I'm giving her the benefit of my experience. Tara, this is way beyond choices—this is about personality types and what can happen. Fern is like I was. We both get hooked into things, obsess about things until we master them, and then move on. Which is fine when the things are positive. But I got hooked into things that I don't want her anywhere near.'

'Oh.'

'Yes—*oh*.'

She would know exactly what he meant. But she still didn't know the extent of it. No one did, really.

'I went down. Crashed. Burned. The lot. Tara, I tried everything—*everything*. Sex, drugs and rock 'n' roll. But I left out the rock 'n' roll.'

She nodded. 'We've all had those offers, Michael. It's part of life. All kids get those offers when they're at any nightclub—it's not just the media kids.'

'Yeah, but when the offers get wilder, and when the people making them are controlling you, supposed to be looking after your interests…'

'Oh.' Again.

The dawning look on her face told him she knew what he meant. And she hadn't been expecting it.

'I lost six months of my life. But I didn't lose myself. That's what I mean about being lucky. No one really knows this, Tara. I had dropped off the face of the earth when I got the news about my mother and Carlos. Their accident. And it came on the front of a newspaper that someone had left lying in a flat I was living in. I think it had been there for two weeks by the time I saw it. I'll never forget the feeling—I thought it was some kind of trip. I couldn't understand it or rationalise it. And I'd missed it—missed my mother's death. I realised that my two baby sisters were completely alone. So somehow I got myself out and I turned myself around. Realised that I had to and, even more, that I *wanted* to protect those that needed protecting. Like Fernanda. And…you.'

'Me? But I don't need protecting from that kind of world—I get offered things, but I know my limits. I know who and what to avoid—I know my way round the scene. I take care of myself. And I would never lead Fern into those situations. *Never.*'

She didn't get it. She just didn't get it.

'I know that. And I'm not saying you need protecting from pimps and pushers. But you need someone at your back. And you seem to bring out that part of me, Tara. You call it control freak? I prefer to call it my sense of responsibility.'

Her eyes were totally wide now.

He smiled at her. 'Yes, *querida*. Whether you like it or not, I'm that kind of guy. Maybe it was the fact that my father sacrificed so much for love, or maybe it was the years with my mother, but it's part of me and, like I said, you bring it out.'

He had to lay it out for her now. Saying the words out loud was making sense to him. He hoped it was making sense to her too.

'And I trust you enough to hold this close. Between us.'

He couldn't stop himself. Did not want to stop himself. So much for keeping it all business. That had lasted—what?—ten minutes max? She was his drug of choice right now. No debate.

He closed the gap and cupped her face, just the way he liked to. Drew the pad of his thumb across her still incredulous mouth. 'I am one lucky guy.'

Her big blue honest eyes were staring right back at him. 'You are… You *are*?'

'Sure. You're such a beautiful woman.' He pulled another kiss from her. Opened his eyes and drank in the scrubbed-clean version of her. 'This face. This body.'

He couldn't get enough—could not stop himself dragging kisses from her, running his hands over her skin, under the robe. But he had to step back. She needed to see what was so obvious—that she was way more than image. She was talented, kind. And much, much softer than she ever made out.

'You're a survivor too, Tara. But your path is narrow—maybe this is a chance to open up. See if there are other ways to be Tara Devine.'

She cast her eyes down again. Her hand went to her hair. Twirling strands round and round. 'This is such a tough call, Michael. Taking me so far out of my comfort zone.'

He shrugged. 'We're looking at options just now. You seemed like a natural fit. But not if you're not comfortable.'

'I need to think about it and…and I don't have enough time to do that. I take risks—but every risk is thought through and measured. I don't know. I don't know…'

'Don't do anything you're not sure of. But, Tara, you need to prioritise some things in your life. You're holding yourself back. And what you started to tell me earlier—about your family, your mother.' She opened her mouth but he shook his head, shushed her. 'You need to deal with that. Or start to deal with it.'

'That was just a comment I made, I don't let that get in the way of anything.'

He couldn't stop the double-take, held his hands up. 'OK. Whatever you say. My only advice, for what it's worth, would be that you might want to book some time and talk it through with someone.'

'It's my business that's important to me,—not what some sad old man thinks about me.'

'The sad old man being your grandfather?'

He watched as her face flushed and tightened.

'He has nothing to do with me or my life any more.'

'Clearly.'

He wanted to shake her. Gripped her arms instead and held her there. 'Tara. You're running so fast, but you can't see that you're still tied down. Take some time—think instead of trying to blast your way through life. You'll get there faster in the end.'

She was retreating. Defending. Right in front of his eyes he could see the walls going up again. She was moving back into her safety zone. And the worst of it was how close she had come to taking a really big step out of it.

'Yeah, well, that's time I can't afford right now. Same as I can't afford to stay here and chew the fat. I need to get going—get this show back on the road.'

He nodded. Maybe this was for the best.

'Of course, baby. No problem. The offer still stands—if you want it. We'll be finalising the schedules quite soon, but don't feel under any pressure.' She looked so uncomfortable, so vulnerable, so desperate to get away. It made him ache for her. 'Tara...'

'I'm fine, Michael. Thanks for the offer. It's a great offer. Ehm… I'm going to head off now. Can you call a cab?'

'The car's here—I'll phone down; it'll be ready to go. Take the car.'

She tried a full smile. He wanted to comfort her but she was away, out the room, off down the hall. Tiny and fragile-looking in the big white robe.

He watched her try and fail to pull off a confident stride. Knew without looking that the emotions would be rolling over her face. Maybe there would be tears in her baby blues. But the heavy black weight in her heart was a definite.

CHAPTER TEN

WITH HER PHONE CHARGED, Tara was confronted with a stream of notifications—texts, tweets and posts. Wow! And one call from home. With voicemail. She ignored it. Could not even *think* about going near that right now.

Lars hadn't been at the party after all, but he was still in town and still looking for assets. You had to love a guy who went shopping on that scale—retail therapy for billionaires. Luckily they needed to offload 'pick-me-up' cash too.

Tara started to read through the stuff on her phone. She'd figured she'd be an easy target on social media for her less than elegant exit from the club with Michael, but she'd totally, *totally* underestimated the volume of traffic it had generated.

Even driving out of the underground car park of Michael's apartment building had been a shocker. The driver had warned her there might be a squad and he'd been right—at least half a dozen snappers had stuck their cameras to the window of the car as it had eased over the ramp. Those pictures—flat hair, bare face and hangover—hadn't appeared yet, but it was probably only a matter of time.

But even without them she seemed to have rocked

straight to the top of the 'what's hot' gossip columns. This was easily the most publicity she'd ever had.

Tara Devine—London's newest It Girl?

She warily opened up the link on a tweet from the bitchiest blogger in town.

> *Answer—no! What's happened to party girl Tara? One week at Camp Cruz and she hits the scene looking like an homage to the Flintstones. Sorry, Tara, but you're def not rockin the It Girl look. Is this what happens when you hook up with a man? Last week you launched a kickass collection to the world. Grown-up Girlpower. This week? The wrong dress, the wrong hair and under the arm of the wrong man. Not sayin' any of us would kick Michael Cruz out of bed, but, girlfriend... what you doin', letting yourself be dragged home like carrion?*

Well, she could have predicted that—but it still hurt. As did the dozen or so posts below it. There was no such thing as bad publicity? *Really?* In her position, with another fashion week to go, she couldn't afford to be making mistakes. She might even have made a Worst Dressed list somewhere. Where was her head at? What had she been thinking? So much for her carefully constructed image. Fashion designers just did *not* make bad fashion choices. She needed to get this sorted. And fast.

The wrong man.

Why on earth had that even got a mention? They were reading so much more into this than was real. Michael wasn't her 'man'. She didn't have room in her life for a man. And there was no doubt in her mind that he didn't see it that way either. He was…

Her mind rolled with images: of herself choking on her drink when she saw him that first time at the after-party, watching him walk away after he'd kissed her, him handing her the glass of rum and laughing at her nervousness as she knocked it back. Staring at their reflection in his bathroom mirror as he held her against him. He was…

He'd been vile. He'd been amazing. He'd been offensive and sweet and kind and loving.

His dark intense eyes as he handed her coffee, held her face in his hands, kissed her…

Then, this morning, sitting on the bed with a glass of water. Offering to film her for a documentary. Asking her about her mother. And listening to her answer.

She breathed in and closed her eyes, letting the memories wash over her.

Him leaning up on his elbows, filling her and gazing into her eyes. Complete. Replete.

He was too much. Too intense. Too close.

He was the last thing she needed.

She scanned more posts.

She needed to clear her head.

There was so much fallout after last night. Could she really blame him for it? Maybe not, but he hadn't helped.

So, the documentary—definitely not. And Lars—definitely.

She jumped up. She just needed to come clean—maybe tweet about wardrobe malfunctions. Laugh at herself online and then get back on the couture wagon.

Slip into something from her current collection and stalk Lars.

There was no way the last ten years were going to be ruined by an ill-chosen dress and a moment of weakness. OK, Michael was more than a moment of weakness—he was a seismic shift who had taken her on and trusted her with so much. He was everything—handsome, smart, the most sexually perfect partner she could ever imagine having. He was kind, trusting. But for these last few days she had lost herself in him. Lost who she really was. And she couldn't afford to do that. Couldn't afford to get knocked any further off track. Couldn't afford to fixate on him or dwell on the past the way he was suggesting.

Everybody knew where they were with Party Tara—especially her.

She braved the phone again and messaged her contacts. Someone had to know where Lars was. Time for favours to be called in.

By the time she emerged from the hotel room where Team Lars were holed up she had a sponsorship deal, a cash-flow solution and an invitation to dinner. Not a bad day's work considering she was so not an It Girl.

She made her way past the super-rich, who were accessorising the various corners of the hotel like throws and silk cushions. Sheikhs, thin women in couture, couples in identical cruise wear, and then the bag lady types—usually the richest of them all.

She skipped along, feeling almost fantastic. A couple of hours' downtime and then on to meet Lars in Soho. She wasn't really sure what his MO was in all of this. He had a lot of cash. He was light on fashion in his portfolio. He had a big interest in her assets. It almost made her squirm. But, hey-ho, she could cope with that and then some.

She took out her phone.

Her breath caught in her throat.

A missed call from Michael. And another call from home. She screwed up her eyes. *Not yet. Please not yet.* She wasn't ready. Just not ready.

An eight-course, wine-matched dining marathon was not quite what she'd had in mind. Her heart sank after the wasabi sorbet, and she was counting the hours until the white chocolate mousse with truffle-roasted hazelnut and blueberry coulis. She could hardly say it, never mind eat it. And by the time she rolled out of here she would have gone up another dress size.

Lars was a sweet kid. That was all she could describe him as. Well, cute. He could be described as cute too. But he was way better suited to someone like Fernanda than to a woman like Tara, who'd lived through two editors of French *Vogue*. When she spent time with a man she wanted it to be someone who'd lived, who was intelligent, who could have a conversation that ran further than television stars and where to park your yacht. But that was way off in the future. Right now she wanted this night to end and her life to settle back down.

She turned her phone over to check for a message. Or a call. Nothing. Good—that was good. She could not cope with anything else right now. Once Paris was in the bag, maybe then she could stop and think. She could maybe meet Michael for lunch?.

Maybe not. *The wrong dress, the wrong hair and under the arm of the wrong man.* She couldn't get that out of her mind. How could something that had felt so right be so wrong? No, better to put distance between them—miles and miles of distance. Focus on the show next week. Get the media focused on that side of Devine Design again. A few photos with Lars would be a good start.

It was when he put his hand on the small of her back that she really began to get annoyed. Getting out of the car to go to yet another function. Walking in and seeing Michael. And wanting to turn and run right back out through the door.

It was a retrospective photography exhibition being held in a cavernous nightclub, and she should have known he would be there. He was with Angelica. He was the most handsome man she had ever seen. He was staring right at her. Even among the giant canvasses of iconic images, huge portraits that seemed to have stunned everyone else, he was like a beacon and she couldn't take her eyes off him.

Lars dragged his hand across her back and looped it over her shoulders. His fingers rested on the top of her breast. Michael's eyes were like missiles. She was pinned to the spot. His jaw was tense and almost totally square. His fabulous, loving mouth was set in an angry line. She could feel the energy from across the room. Angelica placed a hand on his arm, but it was like a blade of grass on a tsunami.

Who the hell did he think he was?

OK, so maybe he'd been expecting her to return his call…but she'd been busy! And agreeing to go to dinner and an exhibition with Lars was actually not a big deal. It was the polite thing to do. It gave her that little bit of distance she needed. And she'd been more than up-front with Michael that she was not going to change who she was and how she did things just because *he* thought she should.

But he'd turned his head and was talking to a group of *his* type of people—all money, class and effortless charm. Wow. She was *so* not part of that scene. Thank god. She was so different from him. Even though there had been times when she'd felt absorbed by him, part of him—as if no one else in the world understood her like him. But that had just been the heat of the moment. No big deal.

She needed a drink. Even with his back to her she could still feel his presence. He was still making her feel that she needed her shield. And her sword. Or her running shoes.

She checked that there was no press. There was no press. But there might be some opportunists. She shrugged her shoulders out of Lars's octopus arm and made her way to…to anywhere other than this public arena.

A few people stopped her, complimented her on her clothes—the red version of the cream satin dress she'd been wearing that first night she'd met Michael. Inlaid with darts of rubber and more than a nod to the fetish scene.

'Wrap that round ya, Cruz,' she muttered to herself.

She moved through the crowd. Fielded a few questions about Lars. Laughed off a few bitchy comments about last night's exit. Tried to bluff out her media thrashing.

The eight matched wines had been small measures, drunk slowly, but there was no doubt that her senses were a bit dulled. She ordered a shot to give her an edge. Lifted the glass to her mouth.

'Tara.'

She let the glass hover, then downed it. Slapped it down on the bar. 'What?'

'You tell *me* what.'

'I'll tell you what, all right.' She knew she was making a mistake taking him on. In public. And after the day that she'd had. But he wasn't her keeper and she had every right to sink a few. 'Thanks to you I've had a fantastic time explaining your caveman tactics from yesterday. *Oh, how we laughed. Oh, how I loved Michael grabbing me up and stuffing me in his car*—said no one—ever.' She nodded to the barman. 'Same again.'

'You don't need another, Tara. You need to go home—preferably with me. You've had a lot to drink and it's been a tough day for you. I've seen the media. I know how you'll be feeling.'

His voice was low, totally uncompromising. Utter control and no room for manoeuvre. But he was dealing with her. Not his sisters. Not his idealised version of a woman who did as she was told.

'Wrong, Michael. You don't know how I'm feeling—you *think* you do, because you think you know everything. But you don't know me. And don't even *think* about laying a finger on me to drag me out of here.'

He was right beside her now. Looking down with that intense dark stare. She turned right round to face him—body to body. And what a body it was. She knew it. She felt drawn in to the energy he radiated. It would be so easy—so gloriously easy to wrap her arms around him and let her mouth tug out those divine kisses. She was right inside his arc of strength. He was everything. No touch but he could twist her to his will.

'I'm not taking you anywhere you don't want to be. But you were in too deep last night and you're heading that way again tonight. And the worst of it is you don't even want to be here—it's obvious. You put on your smile and you put up your hair and the Tara Show comes to town.'

'The Tara Show? Is that what you think I am? A pantomime?'

'I think right now that you're spoiling for a fight. And I don't know why.'

She turned back to the barman, who had lined up her next shot. Truly, the thought of it was making her feel slightly sick.

'I don't want to fight. I just want to be me. And that's not a pantomime—or a show. Until I met you I didn't have any self-doubt. None. I knew where I was going and I knew how to get there. But now? Now I'm questioning every move that I make—every dress that I wear. And I'm getting it all wrong!'

She heard her voice getting more and more high-pitched. Picked up the shot glass. Held it between them. 'I don't even know if I want to sink *this*. That's how you've got me! All over the place. I missed a call with a really high-end fashion editor. I forgot…*forgot*…to get my transport sorted until it was nearly too late! I'm losing control.'

She threw the liquor down her throat and winced as it burned. Slammed the glass down.

'Feel better after that?'

She hiccoughed. 'Much.'

He trailed his finger down her cheek. Warm, soft, tender.

'It doesn't always have to be the hard path, Tara.'

She felt the pull of him. Oh, he was so tempting—she could so easily reach out and touch his chest. Feel his heat and wrap herself up in it. But that wasn't going to help. She needed space and distance—not more closeness.

'I'll be leaving shortly. Angelica is meeting Sebastian and I want you to come with me. Let me look after you, *querida*.'

She rolled her eyes. 'Stop trying to order me about, Michael. Don't you know me by now? That just gets my back up.'

She turned back to the barman. 'Spring me another. Please.'

'Wow, Tara—you're determined to wreck this, aren't you? You're really set on another night like last night—and you know I'm not going to be here to pick up the pieces.'

'I've never needed anyone to pick up after me. I sort things for myself, Michael. No interference necessary. Thanks all the same.'

He held his hands up and stepped back. 'You know where I am and you know what I want. But I'll not bother you again—not while you're working through whatever it is that's eating you alive like this.'

She grasped the shot glass that had been placed before her. Closed fingers round the glass that was already sticky with liquor. Threw it down her throat. Closed her eyes and felt it burn. Coughed. And when she looked round he was gone.

For a moment she wanted to run, to chase after him. She actually felt him withdrawing, leaving, and the force of it hit her hard like another sucker punch. She braced two arms on the bar. Dipped her head. Felt a huge, harsh sob swell from her soul and bit down hard. She couldn't lose it here. She *couldn't.*

She stifled it and swallowed and kept her head low, until she was sure she could walk without her legs buckling. But the tears had gathered—a thick film that swelled over her eyes. She couldn't see where she was going. Two slim arms reached for her, steered her to a corner. Angelica. Hugging her and holding her and shushing her.

'Tara. Go after him. He only wants to do the right thing for you. I know it. I can see it. He loves you. I'm sure he does.'

But Tara shook her head as the tears began to fall. Even if it was true she couldn't let herself open up any more. She had so much riding on these next few days. Her success. Her sanity. What good would it do to go after him? To say sorry? To tell him she loved him? How could she be sure she even knew what love was?

'I can't, Angelica. He's not right for me. He's too much. I can't take that amount of control in my life. I'm the boss of me—not any man. And Michael is more than any man I've ever met—it's who he is. It defines him. I need to be defined by me and me alone. He would swallow me up. I already feel I've lost my way and things are falling apart.'

She squeezed her friend's hand and then slipped out of her grasp. She needed to go now. At least she had figured one thing out—at least she knew now for sure that she was better off alone permanently. All those feelings of leaning on Michael, being absorbed by him and enjoying his strength—so tempting, but so wrong.

She walked to the doors. Squared her shoulders. Wiped her eyes and fixed her smile.

CHAPTER ELEVEN

It was a day like any other. Michael told himself that over and over. If he viewed it as anything else he would risk getting caught up in the hysteria that seemed to have settled like an electric storm over this corner of Catalonia. Thankfully he'd left the house to the girls, so the frenzy was only an imprint rather than the real deal.

He drained his third coffee of the day and looked over at Angelica's fiancé, Sebastian. Pacing. He'd been up for hours and the strain was already beginning to tell. Crazy that people put themselves through this. Actually volunteered to tie themselves in knots—not only in the preparation, but then on the day.

Even the most cool and collected of them all—Angelica—had been showing signs of stress in the past forty-eight hours. And he'd never, ever witnessed that before. Fern, of course, was playing the sulky teenager to perfection. Like a military strategist. Withdrawn, one-word answers, and then without warning she'd flare up and fire a couple of missiles that took everyone by surprise. Maybe he'd been like that at one point. Who knew?

There was so much going on at work too. His phone was permanently in his grasp but he'd cleared everything for what he was determined was going to be a turning point in his life. That seemed to have taken his assistant by surprise, because in the past few months he had agreed to almost everything to do with business.

Nothing better for getting a sense of perspective than to immerse yourself in a new project and bring it home. He wasn't stupid. He knew that his ventures were his way of dissociation from the events that had happened six months earlier. With Tara.

Leaving that photography exhibition without throwing her over his shoulder had been one of the hardest things he'd ever done—he who prided himself on his self-control and on the unflinching compliance of others. But she had to *want* to come. She had to control herself. And he had to let her. Though it had almost killed him.

He could still see her so vividly—standing at that bar, in that red satin dress, looking like every man's fantasy. But only truly totally his. And the way she'd been knocking back those shots, as if every one was underlining more and more the Tara she wanted the world to see.

He had ached to take her in his arms, to show her with his body that she was so much more. To tell her that it was her courage that he loved, her wit, her passion. Her heart. But she might never have forgiven him if he'd acted the caveman again. He hadn't been able to risk that. He'd had to give her the space she needed. So there had been no alternative—he'd had to walk away. And that had really, truly taught him a lesson.

It had taken some solid hours of his life. Alone. Working through who he thought he was and who he thought *she* was. Coming to terms with the fact that she wasn't going to roll up at his door and beg him to let her in. Battling with himself to stay away—because he really couldn't trust himself not to use his body, their red-hot sexual chemistry, to get her to submit to what he wanted—which was her in his life for ever.

He'd had to come to terms also with the fact that the issues that were in her mind might never be fixed. There was a lot buried inside that beautiful head of hers. Maybe too deeply buried. He'd had time to piece together the little she'd told him. Growing up as an unwanted baby, her mother's guilty secret, in a house ruled by fear. If that was what she had suffered throughout her childhood it was going to take an awful lot of love to put right. All he could hope was that she had left the door open wide enough for that still to happen. And that it was him she was going to let in. The part he had to master was his almost pathological need to break it down and force her to see that.

She could not and would not let anyone do anything to help. Unless she decided it for herself.

So it was a question of timing. She would work this stuff out. One day. But life moved on. She might meet someone else—someone who would be there when she finally crossed the emotional rivers she swam in to reach the other side. But how long until she was ready for that? He had seen enough of life to know that you couldn't force that kind of personal growth. Would she still be single when it all fell into place for her? Would she wait for him?

But he had faith. And he believed in luck. Believed you made your own, and Tara seemed to be doing just that.

He flicked through the apps on his phone. His guilty

secret. After the small successes of her shows over the last few months things had really begun to take off. She had a blog now, for fashion TV, and he sometimes—OK often—read it. It was his way of keeping an eye on her while still keeping his distance. Giving her space. And she was good. She was developing her profile appropriately, in a way that suited her and that she clearly had control over. Her fan base had swelled and she seemed to be getting more credibility as a designer.

And that was what she needed. She needed approval and validation from people she respected. Fair enough. That was a natural reaction. One day she would realise that it was approval and validation from herself that would show she really had moved on. He hoped for her sake that that day wasn't too far ahead.

He scanned the blog. It said it all.

Summed up the craziness of what he was about to walk into.

Wedding of the Season: Angelica Cruz and Sebastian Frietze. In less than twenty-four hours the legendary Catalonian beauty and heiress will marry her long-time sweetheart Seb Frietze.

You've all been waiting to see why a goddess like Angelica would choose to ask a demonia-devotee such as myself to design the dress for her very, very special day, and all I can say is... wait and see! I'm not gonna lie and say that she's going to shimmy her way down the aisle in rubber or latex, and the wedding favours are not going to be handcuffs, but she's pushed some very important boundaries, girls!

And as for her bridesmaid, Fernanda? Let's

say you'd better clear your diaries for the whole of next week as you check out the online frenzy that's going to follow this teenage idol. Oh, and finally, there's no truth in the rumour that the men will be wearing gimp masks.

She was a little witch. He had no doubt that that was a prod at him rather than Sebastian. A dig at his 'ultra-conservative' image that she had taken great delight in ripping him for. He smiled. Flicked the photo on the screen larger. Seeing her winking by-line photo grin up at him, he smiled even more broadly. How he loved that face. He loved the mocking intelligence in her eyes. He loved her quirky teeth and the way her face tilted so happily with her smile. He loved those lips, those kisses. Man, how he missed her kisses. Missed her. Ached for her. Loved her.

When had he known? He'd asked himself that over and over. So many flashbacks of so many treasured moments. But it had been when she was least 'Tara'—when she had been stripped of everything she thought made her who she was—no super-styled hair, no make-up, no crazy clothes. When she had been in his kitchen dressed in that huge white robe. Just a person. The most adorable person in the world.

Well, Ms Devine—I'll be seeing you soon enough, he thought. And he knew he had everything riding on getting this just right. He'd stayed out of the way while she was scooping up the rewards of Fashion Week. He'd given her all the space she needed to forge more success with her business. And he'd stayed well away from all the talk about her carefully orchestrated by Angelica.

He'd even withstood the temptation to catch her at

the house before she made last-minute adjustments to the dresses, but in less than two hours he was going to be face to face with her. And he was determined. This would be nailed. Finally.

Tara's fingers were sausages. Her head was soup—and not consommé. Angelica stood before her, Fernanda and her phone sat at the side of her—and if she was on social media she was going to be toast.

She knew that this was the design of her life. And she couldn't have dreamed up a better model to showcase it. Angelica's classical beauty was the perfect foil for the slightly *outré* but totally feminine dress that she had designed. On anyone else it would be too corseted, too burlesque, too much. On Tara herself it would look like she was auditioning for the lead as *Bride of Frankenstein*, but on Angelica it looked truly divine.

She should be content. Excited, but content. It was the culmination of weeks of collaboration and fittings. But it was excitement at seeing the other Cruz sibling that was eating her alive. She couldn't believe Michael had walked out of her life like that. She'd been so sure that he'd come over all caveman and drag her off later that night, or at least in the days that followed. She'd begun to prime herself to accept that that was just his way, and that she should swallow her horror and maybe come to terms with it.

But he hadn't come back. Hadn't called, texted or in any way made contact. Had left her with a massive gap that came from the immense physical and emotional contact that had been withdrawn, turned off, extinguished. And she had hurt. So badly. Not even the amount of business her sales agent had managed to generate with stores all round Europe had completely erased the bleakness she felt. Just putting one foot in front of the other and breathing had become harder than she'd ever have thought possible.

Still, she had taken the time to really work herself out. And that hadn't been pretty. At all…

The make-up artist and hairdressers were finishing off. She had declined to let them near herself—she'd already lived through one of those disasters, when Angelica's hairdresser had thought he understood her look and she'd had to pull the whole lot out and fix it herself later. No, the last thing she could afford to look today was anything other than lovely.

Her own dress was also new. Showcasing a new mood, a new muse. A new understanding of her own femininity and personality. And she'd be lying if she said she hadn't designed it knowing Michael's eyes were going to fall on it.

In approximately two hours.

Sebastian's anxiety was viral. Michael had contracted a severe case of pacing and hand-wringing himself now. And even standing at the foot of the stairs, waiting for Angelica to descend with her one bridesmaid and her one dress designer, he could only be grateful that he was hidden from the sight of the two hundred or so of Angelica's 'close' friends—aka projects—who had gathered in their garden to watch this wedding.

And of course she was going to be late—more hand-wringing—and it would be hours before he got a chance to speak to Tara alone. To see where they were going. And to make sure it was together.

He heard a noise from upstairs. Felt tension and excitement waft down to him like heavy perfume. Top notes of high-pitched voices and hints of hysteria. He began to feel—actually, was it flu coming on? This was so, *so* not like him.

And there they were. His sister looked stunning. Truly he'd never seen Angelica look so beautiful. And even Fernanda was more breathtaking than usual. But it was the small strawberry blonde behind them that his eyes searched for. And as his sisters moved downstairs and Tara finally came into view it was her blue eyes that found his. And the world felt better

With every step that she took he locked her with his eyes. He told her he loved her. He'd missed her. He told her she was not going to get away from him again without a fight. He never let his gaze falter for a second until he had to stretch out his arms to his sister. And then he looked at Angelica with pride. Because this was her day. And he was her brother. And he would do everything he could to make sure she got the best start to her married life.

Angelica beamed. A tear was in her eye. She stood at the foot of the stairs and let Tara reassemble her train. She looked voluptuous, like a goddess, a screen siren—he'd never seen her that way.

And as Tara stood, finally content with the way each layer of dove-white satin and antique lace was lying, Angelica, ambassadorial as ever, took their hands. 'I'm so, so happy you're both here for this day.'

Tara looked at him. Strong, but fragile—sure, yet open. Her perfect porcelain skin was lush with health and he wanted her more than life itself. She nodded the truth of her heart into his eyes and he braced himself to do this duty for Angelica. They would have their time to sort out the words that needed to be said soon enough.

Tara was basking in the comments from the guests. She was basking in Angelica's joy and Fernanda's happiness. And she was absolutely luxuriating in the attention she was getting from Michael. He hadn't taken his eyes off her all day—since she'd seen him at the foot of the stairs, looking as if he'd been cast from the most enchanted spell. He was more than handsome, more powerful, stronger, more solid, cleverer, kinder than anyone she had ever known. And she knew that just by breathing the same air as him.

He walked towards her now and she knew that their moment was coming.

'Tara.'

She put down her champagne flute carefully, untouched, not even a lipstick stain on it.

'I've missed you.'

He stepped up close and placed first one slow kiss, then another on each of her cheeks. He circled her waist with his hand and he made her feel simply cherished.

'I've missed you too.'

She allowed herself to be led to a corner. There were guests milling all over the house. A buffet was on offer and the joy of the day was still in its infancy. Her duties were done but his were stretching out ahead. This moment was going to be short, but she would know how his heart lay.

'You look…simply beautiful.'

She sat down beside him, still not taking her eyes off him. His skin was paler without its summer tan, but his lips were dark as red wine and his eyes were a warm, rich brown. She scanned his face and saw fine laughter lines, involuntarily trailed her fingers there.

'It's so…so good to see you, Michael.'

He took her hand from his face, held it to his mouth, turned it round and kissed her open palm. All the hot, physical love she had missed rose and bubbled immediately, shocking her with its intensity. And he read that and smiled at the gasp she had released.

'It's been too long, *querida*. But we both needed the space.'

'Did we?'

It didn't feel like that to her. It had felt like she was incomplete. Especially since she had waited and waited for him to contact her. And that just hadn't happened.

'I was sure you were going to get in touch. In fact I was sure you were going to haul me off to your cave.'

She laughed and he smiled, turning her hand over in his, enclosing her fingers, trailing his thumb across the veins of her wrist.

'It's not that I didn't think about it. Maybe daily—maybe every hour on the hour.'

He smiled into her eyes and she had to know—had to wonder if their intoxicating kisses were going to be as good as in her dreams. She bent forward into his space, closed her eyes and felt the firm seal of his lips. She moulded her mouth and slipped her tongue to taste him. It was better than good. It was hot. It was perfect. She pushed her chest forward and reached out to touch him. Felt the firm ridge of his biceps where her hands landed lightly on his arms.

'I wish you had. How I wish you had.'

She felt him cup her face, holding her just out of reach as he looked at her. He'd done this before and then she'd taken it as a sign that he was withdrawing. This time she knew that he was only savouring, reading her, learning,

'Tara, if I had done that you might have come, but you would have resented me for it.'

'It would have put me out of my misery.'

'I know—and it would have ended mine. But you're not a trophy, and I'm not looking for that in my woman. I need someone strong, independent. I need a match, Tara, not a princess.'

Really? She smiled. Then that was a total turnaround. It sounded like the right words, but she couldn't see the Michael Cruz she knew really meaning them.

'Michael. You're the most dominant man I've ever known—just think back to the very first time we met. At the after-party. Fernanda was hiding from you and Angelica was using me as a decoy. And you seduced me—swept me off my feet so much that I was happy to jump into bed with you. That's not the behaviour of an equal rights activist in touch with his feminine side.'

He chuckled briefly. 'Well, let's not labour the "in touch with my feminine side" part too much—let's call that an objective rather than an actuality. But you're right. OK. In some ways, yes, you're right.'

Well, this was progress. She'd never expected to hear those sentiments coming out of his mouth.

'But you've also got to remember that I was, and still am, responsible for a girl who has diva potential in every pore of her being. If I hadn't taken a hard line with Fernanda who knows what kind of nonsense she'd be up to? It's hard enough, Tara. But she takes a lot of work—as you know.'

'Like her big brother.'

He leaned in for a gorgeous, long, sensual kiss and she melted right there.

'I'm a pussycat where you're concerned.'

'Now you're just being ridiculous. And you know that I no more want a pussycat than you want a hard-ass bitch.'

'Sounds like we might be learning to compromise, then.'

He kissed her again. Melted what was left. Someone approached them—Sebastian.

'Michael, I'm sorry to interrupt, but Angelica is asking for you?'

For a moment he looked as if he wasn't going to move, or he hadn't heard. Then his face softened. 'I'll be right there.' He ran his hands up and down her arms. 'I have to finish this for Angelica and Seb. But I want us to have time to talk. Properly talk. Without our lust for each other getting in the way. I mean that, Tara. I think it's really important for us to clear up the stuff that's plagued us up until now. Hmm?'

She nodded. Really, the last thing she wanted to do was talk if there was even half a chance of getting naked any time soon. She'd never thought she had a high sex drive before, but sitting here without ripping his clothes off was a real test of character.

'I'm not going anywhere. I'll be here when you're ready. We've got a lovely day ahead with Angel and Seb, and I'm just so glad to be here to share it with them.'

'Good, baby. That's good. We'll have plenty of time later.' He gave her another drugging kiss and then stood up.

She watched him walk away, so tall, so erect, so in control of the whole room, of his whole world.

She felt the back of her hair. A couple of pins had fallen out of her loose French roll. Why was she such a slave to fashion? If Mario and the guys she used for her shows had said *tight* French rolls were in she would have backcombed, pinned and sprayed like a fiend. And then she wouldn't have had to worry about her hair all day. Loose French rolls? One of fashion's more stupid ideas.

She stood up and went upstairs to her room. She could check her messages, maybe even have a glass of iced tea and change her shoes. The day couldn't be going any better.

She closed the door of the guest bedroom and headed to the dressing table. Started to undo the remaining couple of pins from her hair and kicked off her heels. They were beautiful. They were a quid pro quo promotion by a colleague she was in partnership with, and they'd served their purpose, but no way was she going to last the day in them.

Her phone sounded. She glanced at it. She would get it in a minute.

She moved to the mirror, looked at herself. Although he hadn't commented, Michael couldn't have failed to notice the change in her. Everyone else had. She was still Tara Devine, but she was just a bit less full-on, a bit softer. Her designs this season were still super-flattering for curves, and still oozed sex appeal, but she liked to think she'd found dignity and an air of mystery…even if it was just an inch lower on the hem and higher on the cleavage. It was something to keep the critics in column inches anyway.

Her phone sounded again. She picked it up. The screen was covered in messages. She held it in her hand and looked at them all. There was no ignoring it this time. Missed calls. Texts. And she knew without even opening them up what they were about.

She sank onto the bed. The last contact had been to tell her that he was ill and ask if she wanted to come home. Were they out of their minds? she had said. Another couple of attempts had been made.

Maybe it was the way she had been feeling about Michael, although she doubted it, but she had almost, *almost* spoken about it. Had wondered if it was time and had actually looked up a therapist's phone number. Maybe she should now. Maybe she would. There was no doubt it was all going to come to the surface now. No doubt that something serious had happened. And no doubt she would have to deal with it…

It was only when the door opened that she realised how long she had been sitting there. It was Michael. He walked to her. There was no need to discuss anything. He just knew. Just his being in the room consoled her. And she felt another part of the dark shadow within her fade and die.

'Tara? What's wrong?'

He scooped her into his arms and she sat there numbly. Just being held. Words were in her heart somewhere, but she couldn't feel them or properly form them yet. He soothed her and held her close. Maybe it was the beat of his heart—slow, steady, reassuring. Maybe it was how far she'd come already herself on her journey. But she knew that she was going to get past this.

She swallowed. Tried to sit up. 'Just some news from home.'

He looked at her closely. She felt such a wave of love from him. Returned it. She didn't even need to say the words—she just knew how he treasured her. There were so many more important things for them to fix than any old skeletons in her closet. They needed to talk about practical things—like how he was going to cope with her moods when she had one of her catastrophising fits when stylists totally misinterpreted her fifties fetish in a Thunderbird vision in her latest ad campaign, or when make-up artists put far too much smudge into her 'slept in my mascara' catwalk look. What was wrong with people that they didn't get that? These were the kinds of things that could really bring her down.

'Tara, any news from home, or anything else you want to share with me, I'm here for you, *querida*.'

He looked so concerned. And it was like drinking an elixir. She reached out and cupped his cheek, kissed his lips.

'I know, Michael. I know. And truly, truly, I will tell you everything. We'll fix this together. Just not today. Not on Angelica's special day.' She had to have his mouth then. Had to feel the force of his love around her. 'Do you think anyone would miss you for ten minutes?'

'Tara, I think they're surprised I've not disappeared before now. But we promised we would talk. We *should* talk.' He gripped her face and took her mouth. 'But I can't get enough of you. I'll never have enough of you.'

She felt almost overwhelmed by the force of his kiss. But she gave it right back.

'Tara, I love you. I haven't told you yet.'

'You didn't need to. I can see it. I can feel it. You've wrapped me up in it. I love you too, by the way.'

He laughed and showered her face with more kisses. 'Yeah?'

'Yeah. But we still need to agree who's the boss.'

'No contest. You are.'

She grinned. 'Really? *Really?*'

He grinned back. 'Well, unless you step out of line. Then I might have to get physical.'

He kissed her in between each word. Pushed her back down on the bed.

'This kind of physical I can deal with. As long as you know that I'm still going to be the boss.'

The pull of their mutual desire was huge. It had been building for all these months and she had to let it take over. Had to be imprinted on him, had to breathe his air and learn his body all over again.

She flipped round, lifted her skirts past her thighs and straddled him. He lay back on the bed, undid his trousers and pulled out his hot, heavy erection. She shifted her tiny pants to the side as it stiffened in her hand. Looked at him. He reached up to her face, cupped it the way she liked him to. She turned her head and kissed his palm—and then they could wait no longer. He filled her. She filled him. Love and passion in balance.

'I only want this. Only this. You and me. For ever.'

He touched her, made love to her, and she knew then that every last demon was exorcised. She had no need to defend herself. No need to fight. No need to fear. He turned her round, slipped his arms under her and held her close while he rocked them both to their peak. And when they finally lay together, entwined in hot limbs and breath and happiness, she whispered her love to him over and over.

A total connection. A total partnership. Totally true.

EPILOGUE

By the time the last of the models had done her final turn Tara was ready to make the trek herself. She linked arms with Fernanda, and Angelica, her most special guest. Angelica's agreement to model some of her new bridal collection had been the total icing on the wedding cake after the media furore generated by her first bridal design. The plans she had begun to sketch for her own dress were still strictly private, and even though she now shared everything with Michael this was one design he would only see on the day itself—in six months' time.

She smiled at her girlfriends. What a team.

Fernanda was easily the most marketable model she'd ever known: a darling with the press and muse of one of the most famous French fashion houses. And all of that fitted in with her studies, just to be sensible. Angelica's new role with UNICEF was keeping her very busy, but Tara was sure there would be other more personal news she would be sharing soon. There was no way her waist had thickened like that by itself.

Some terrifying people had attended today, but the immediate reaction had been positive and the knot in her stomach had loosened and shifted. She squeezed her *amigas*, stepped forward and paused.

Polite applause and raucous cheers. And there in the front row was her darling, her Michael. Easily the most handsome man in the room, and putting his charm to good use sitting beside one of the most formidable fashionistas, who looked actually—happy!

She stepped out, keeping pace as best she could with the long-limbed beauties. And as Michael's eyes caught hers, as they always did and always would, the euphoria she felt at her success was redoubled by the knowledge of his pride and their love. She winked at him and he beamed right back.

She toured past him, down and back up. He was with her every step of the way, showing the world and, more importantly, showing her that even though he still preferred to dress like a boring banker, as she called it, he could appreciate her art and her creativity.

Which was just as well because, oh, yes, she thought, *she* was the boss. But later she hoped he would get as physical as possible—just to keep her guessing.

* * * * *